CRIME IN THE CAFE

BOOKS BY FIONA GRACE

LACEY DOYLE COZY MYSTERY
MURDER IN THE MANOR (Book#1)
DEATH AND A DOG (Book #2)
CRIME IN THE CAFE (Book #3)
VEXED ON A VISIT (Book #4)
KILLED WITH A KISS (Book #5)
PERISHED BY A PAINTING (Book #6)
SILENCED BY A SPELL (Book #7)
FRAMED BY A FORGERY (Book #8)
CATASTROPHE IN A CLOISTER (Book #9)

TUSCAN VINEYARD COZY MYSTERY
AGED FOR MURDER (Book #1)
AGED FOR DEATH (Book #2)
AGED FOR MAYHEM (Book #3)

DUBIOUS WITCH COZY MYSTERY
SKEPTIC IN SALEM: AN EPISODE OF MURDER (Book #1)
SKEPTIC IN SALEM: AN EPISODE OF CRIME (Book #2)
SKEPTIC IN SALEM: AN EPISODE OF DEATH (Book #3)

BEACHFRONT BAKERY COZY MYSTERY
BEACHFRONT BAKERY: A KILLER CUPCAKE (Book #1)
BEACHFRONT BAKERY: A MURDEROUS MACARON (Book #2)
BEACHFRONT BAKERY: A PERILOUS CAKE POP (Book #3)

CRIME IN THE CAFE

(A Lacey Doyle Cozy Mystery-Book 3)

FIONA GRACE

FIONA GRACE

Debut author Fiona Grace is author of the LACEY DOYLE COZY MYSTERY series, comprising nine books (and counting); of the TUSCAN VINEYARD COZY MYSTERY series, comprising three books (and counting); of the DUBIOUS WITCH COZY MYSTERY series, comprising three books (and counting); and of the BEACHFRONT BAKERY COZY MYSTERY series, comprising three books (and counting).

Fiona would love to hear from you, so please visit www.fionagrace-author.com to receive free ebooks, hear the latest news, and stay in touch.

TABLE OF CONTENTS

CHAPTER ONE

"Hey, Lacey!" came Gina's voice from the back room of the antiques store. "Come here a minute."

Lacey gently placed the antique brass candelabra she'd been polishing onto the counter. The soft thud it emitted caused Chester, her English Shepherd, to quirk his head up.

He'd been sleeping in his usual spot, stretched across the floorboards beside the counter, bathed in a beam of June sunshine. He tipped his dark brown eyes up to Lacey, and his tufty eyebrows twitched with evident curiosity.

"Gina needs me," Lacey told him, his perceptive expression always making her feel as if he could understand every word she said. "You keep an eye on the store and bark if any customers come in. Got it?"

Chester whinnied his acknowledgment and sank his head back onto his paws.

Lacey headed through the archway that separated the main shop floor from the large, recently converted auction room. It was the shape of a train carriage—long and narrow—but the ceiling stretched high like that of a church.

Lacey loved this room. But then again, she loved everything about her store, from the retro furniture section she'd used her past knowledge as a New York City interior designer's assistant to curate, to the vegetable garden out back. The store was her pride and joy, even if at times she felt it brought her more trouble than it was worth.

She entered through the arch, and a warm breeze came in through the open back door, bringing with it fragrant smells from the flower garden Gina had been cultivating. But the woman herself was nowhere to be seen.

Lacey scanned the auction room, then deduced Gina must have been calling to her from the garden, and headed in the direction of the open French doors. But as she went, she heard a shuffling noise coming from the left-hand corridor.

The corridor housed the more unsightly parts of her store—the cramped office filled with filing cabinets and steel safes; the kitchen area where her faithful kettle and variety of caffeinated beverages lived; the bathroom (or "loo" as everyone in Wilfordshire referred to it), and the boxy storage room.

"Gina?" Lacey called into the darkness. "Where are you?"

"Cooey!" came her friend's voice, muffled as if she had her head in something. Knowing Gina, she probably did. "I'm in the storeroom!"

Lacey frowned. There was no reason for Gina to be in the storeroom. A condition of Lacey employing her was that she wouldn't overexert herself with any heavy lifting. But then again, when did Gina ever listen to anything Lacey said?

With a sigh, Lacey went down the corridor and into the storeroom. She found Gina crouching in front of the shelving unit, her frazzled gray hair piled on top of her head in a bun fixed with a purple velvet scrunchie.

"What are you doing back here?" Lacey asked her friend.

Gina swiveled her head to look up at her. She'd recently invested in a pair of red-framed glasses, claiming they were "all the rage in Shoreditch" (though why a sixty-plus-year-old pensioner would take her fashion cues from the trendy youths of London was beyond Lacey) and they slid down her nose. She used an index finger to push them back into place, then pointed at an oblong cardboard box on the shelf in front of her.

"There's an unopened box here," Gina announced. Then, with a knowingly conspiratorial tone, she added, "And the postmark says it's from Spain."

Lacey immediately felt her cheeks warm. The parcel was from Xavier Santino, the handsome Spanish antiques collector who'd attended her nautical-themed auction the previous month, in an attempt to reunite his family's collection of lost heirlooms. Along with Lacey, he'd ended up becoming a suspect in the murder of an American tourist. They'd become friendly during the ordeal, their bond cemented further by Xavier's coincidental connection to her missing father.

"It's just something Xavier sent me," Lacey said, trying to brush it off. "You know he's helping me piece together information about my father's disappearance."

Gina rose from her crouch, knees cricking, and peered at Lacey with a suspicious gaze. "I know very well what he's supposed to be doing," she said, her hands going to her hips. "What I don't understand is why he's sending you gifts. That's the third this month."

"Gifts?" Lacey retorted defensively, picking up on Gina's insinuation. "An envelope filled with receipts from my father's store during Xavier's trip to New York hardly constitutes a gift in my eyes."

Gina's expression remained nonplussed. She tapped her foot. "What about the painting?"

In her mind's eye, Lacey pictured the oil painting of a boat at sea that Xavier had mailed her just last week. She'd hung it above the fireplace in her living room at Crag Cottage.

"It's the type of boat his great-great-grandfather captained," she told Gina, defensively. "Xavier found it in a flea market and thought I might like it." She gave a nonchalant shrug, trying to downplay it.

"Huh," Gina grunted, her lips pressed into a straight line. "*Saw this and thought of you.* You know how that looks to an outsider…"

Lacey huffed. She'd reached the end of her patience. "Whatever you're hinting at, why don't you just come out and say it?"

"Fine," her friend replied boldly. "I think there's more to Xavier's gift-giving than you're willing to accept. I think he likes you."

Though Lacey had guessed her friend was implying as much, she still felt affronted hearing it spoken so plainly.

"I'm perfectly happy with Tom," she argued, her mind's eye conjuring up an image of the gorgeous, broad-smiled baker she was lucky enough to call her lover. "Xavier's only trying to help. He promised he would when I gave him his great-grandfather's sextant. You're just inventing drama where there is none."

"If there was no drama," Gina replied calmly, "then why are you hiding Xavier's parcel on the bottom shelf of the storage cupboard?"

Lacey faltered momentarily. Gina's accusations had taken her off guard and left her flustered. For a moment, she forgot the reason why she'd stowed the parcel away after signing for the delivery, instead of opening it right away. Then she remembered; the paperwork was delayed. Xavier had said she'd need to sign an accompanying certificate, so she'd decided to stow it away for the time being in case she accidentally violated any finickity British law she'd yet to learn. With the amount of time the police had ended up sniffing around her store, she couldn't really be too careful!

"I'm not hiding it," Lacey said. "I'm waiting for the certification to arrive."

"You don't know what's inside?" Gina asked. "Xavier didn't tell you what it was?"

Lacey shook her head.

"And you didn't ask?" her friend prompted.

Again, Lacey shook her head.

She noticed then that the look of accusation in Gina's eyes was starting to fade. Instead, it was being overtaken with curiosity.

"Do you think it could be something…" Gina lowered her voice. "…illegal?"

Despite being confident Xavier had not shipped her some banned item, Lacey was more than happy to divert the topic away from his gift, so she ran with it.

"Could be," she said.

Gina's eyes widened further. "What kind of things?" she asked, sounding like an awed child.

"Ivory, for one," Lacey told her, recalling knowledge from her studies of items that were illegal to sell in the UK, antiques or otherwise. "Anything made from the fur of an endangered species. Upholstery made with fabric that's not fire-retardant. Obviously weapons…"

All hints of suspicion now entirely vacated Gina's expression; the "drama" over Xavier was forgotten in the blink of an eye with the far more exciting possibility of there being a weapon inside the box.

"A weapon?" Gina repeated, a little squeak in her voice. "Can't we open it and see?"

She looked as excited as a child beside the tree on Christmas Eve.

Lacey hesitated. She'd been excited to look inside the parcel ever since it had arrived by special courier. It must have cost Xavier an arm and a leg to send it all the way from Spain, and the packaging was elaborate as well; the thick cardboard was as sturdy as wood, and the whole thing was fixed with industrial-sized staples and tied with zip ties. Whatever was inside was obviously very precious.

"Okay," Lacey said, feeling rebellious. "What harm can a peek do?"

She tucked an unruly strand from her dark bangs behind her ear and fetched the box cutter. She used it to slice the zip ties and prize out the staples. Then she opened up the box and sifted through the Styrofoam packaging.

"It's a case," she said, tugging on the leather handle and heaving out a heavy wooden case. Styrofoam bits fluttered everywhere.

"Looks like a spy's briefcase," Gina said. "Oh, you don't think your father was a spy, do you? Maybe a Russian one!"

Lacey rolled her eyes as she placed the heavy case onto the floor. "I may have entertained a lot of outlandish theories about what happened to my father over the years," she said, clicking open the catches of the case one after the next. "But Russian spy has never been one of them."

She pushed up the lid and looked into the case. She gasped at the sight of what it contained. A beautiful antique flintlock hunting rifle.

Gina started cough-choking. "You can't have that thing in here! Goodness, you probably can't have it in England, full stop! What on earth was Xavier thinking sending this to you?"

But Lacey wasn't listening to her friend's outburst. Her attention was fixated on the rifle. It was in excellent shape, despite the fact it had to be well over a hundred years old.

Carefully, Lacey removed it from the case, feeling the weight of it in her hands. There was something familiar about it. But she'd never held a rifle, much less fired one, and despite the odd sense of déjà vu that had rippled through her, she had no concrete memories to attach to it.

Gina started flapping her hands. "Lacey, put it back! Put it back! I'm sorry I made you take it out. I didn't really think it would be a weapon."

"Gina, calm down," Lacey told her.

But her friend was on a roll. "You need a license! You might even be committing an offense having it in this country at all! Things are very different over here than they are in the USA!"

Gina's squeaking reached a fever pitch but Lacey just left her to it. She'd learned there was no talking Gina down from her panicky outbursts. They always ran their course eventually. Either that, or Gina would tire herself out.

Besides, Lacey's attention was too absorbed by the beautiful rifle to pay her any heed. She was mesmerized by the strange feeling of familiarity it had stirred within her.

She peered down the barrel. Felt the weight of it. The shape of it in her hands. Even the smell of it. There was just something wonderful about the rifle, like it was always meant to belong to her.

Just then, Lacey became aware of silence. Gina had finally stopped ranting. Lacey glanced up at her.

"Are you finished?" she asked, calmly.

Gina was still staring at the rifle like it was a circus tiger escaped from its cage, but she nodded slowly.

"Good," Lacey said. "What I was trying to tell you is that I've not only done my homework on the UK's laws on possession and use of firearms, but I actually have a certificate to legally trade antique ones."

Gina paused, a small, perplexed frown appearing in the space between her brows. "You do?"

"Yes," Lacey assured her. "Back when I was valuing the contents of Penrose Manor, the estate had a whole collection of shooting rifles. I had to apply for a license immediately in order to hold the auction. Percy Johnson helped me organize it all."

Gina pursed her lips. She was wearing her surrogate mother expression. "Why didn't I know about this?"

"Well, you didn't work for me back then, did you? You were just the lady next door whose sheep kept trespassing on my property." Lacey chuckled at the fond memory of her first morning waking up in Crag Cottage to find a herd of sheep munching her grass.

Gina didn't return the smile. She seemed to be in a stubborn mood.

"Still," she said, folding her arms, "you'll need to get it registered with the police, won't you? Have it logged on the firearms database."

At the mention of the police, an image of Superintendent Karl Turner's stern, emotionless face appeared in Lacey's mind's eye, followed quickly by the face of his stoic partner, Detective Inspector Beth Lewis. She'd had enough encounters with the two of them to last a lifetime.

"Actually, I don't," she told Gina. "It's an antique and not in working order. That means it's classified as an ornament. I told you, I already did my homework!"

But Gina wasn't budging. She seemed determined to find fault in the matter.

"Not in working order?" she repeated. "How do you know that for sure? I thought you said the paperwork was delayed."

Lacey hesitated. Gina had her there. She hadn't seen the paperwork yet, so she couldn't be one hundred percent certain the rifle wasn't in working order. But there was no ammunition included in the case, for one thing, and Lacey was quite confident Xavier wouldn't send her a loaded gun through the postal system!

"Gina," she said in a firm but final voice, "I promise you I've got it all under control."

The affirmation rolled easily off Lacey's tongue. She did not know it at the time, but they were words she would soon come to regret ever having uttered.

Gina seemed to relent, though she didn't look too happy about it. "Fine. If you say you've got it covered, then you've got it covered. But why would Xavier send you a bloody *gun* of all things?"

"Now *that* is a good question," Lacey said, suddenly wondering the same thing herself.

She reached inside the parcel and found a folded piece of paper at the bottom. She took it out. Gina's insinuation earlier that Xavier had more than just friendship on his mind made her instantly awkward. She cleared her throat as she unfolded the letter and read it aloud.

"Dear Lacey,

"As you know, I was in Oxford recently ..."

7

She paused, feeling Gina's gaze on her sharpen, as if her friend was silently judging her. Feeling her cheeks grow warm, Lacey maneuvered the letter so as to block Gina from view.

"As you know, I was in Oxford recently searching for my great-grandfather's lost antiques. I saw this rifle, and it jogged my memory. Your father had a similar rifle for sale in his New York store. We talked about it. He told me he had recently been on a hunting trip in England. It was a funny story. He said he had not known, but it was the off-season during his trip, and so he could only legally hunt rabbits. I researched hunting seasons in England, and the off-season is during the summer. I do not recall him saying Wilfordshire by name, but remember you said that was where he holidayed in the summers? Perhaps there is a local hunting group? Perhaps they may have known him?

"Yours, Xavier."

Lacey avoided Gina's scrutinizing glare as she folded up the letter. The older woman didn't even need to speak for Lacey to know what she was thinking—that Xavier could've told her about the memory in a text message, rather than going so overblown as to send her a rifle! But Lacey didn't really care. She was more interested in the contents of the letter than any possible romantic notions underpinning Xavier's actions.

So her father enjoyed *hunting* during his summers in England, did he? That was news to her! Beyond the fact she had no memories of him even owning a rifle, she couldn't imagine her mother being okay with it. She was extremely squeamish. Easily offended. Was that why he'd traveled to a different country to do it? It could've been a secret he'd kept from her mother entirely, a guilty pleasure he only indulged in once a year. Or maybe he'd come over to England to shoot because of the company he kept over here ...

Lacey recalled the beautiful woman in the antiques store, the one who'd helped Naomi after she broke the ornament, the one they'd met again in the streets, when a sunburst behind her head had obscured her features. The woman with the gentle English accent and the fragrant smell. Could she have been the one who'd introduced her father to the hobby? Was it a pastime they shared?

She grabbed her cell to message her younger sister, but only got as far as writing, *"Did Dad own guns ..."* when she was interrupted by Chester *yip-yip-yipping* to get her attention. The bell over the front door must have tinkled.

She returned the rifle to its case, clipping shut the latches, and went to head back to the shop floor.

"You can't leave that lying around!" Gina cried, switching from suspicion back to panic mode in an instant.

"Put it in the safe then, if it concerns you that much," Lacey said over her shoulder.

"Me?" she heard Gina shrilly exclaim.

Though she was already halfway along the corridor, Lacey paused. She sighed.

"I'll be with you in a minute!" she called out in the direction she'd been heading.

Then she turned, went back into the storeroom, and picked up the case.

As she carried it past Gina, the woman kept her cautious gaze locked on it and stepped back as if it might explode at any second. Lacey managed to wait until she'd fully passed before rolling her eyes at Gina's overly dramatic reaction.

Lacey took the rifle to the large steel safe where her most precious and expensive items were safely locked away, and secured it inside. Then she headed back into the corridor, where a meek-looking Gina followed her to the shop floor. At least now that the gun was out of sight, she'd finally stopped squawking.

Back on the main shop floor, Lacey was expecting to see a customer perusing one of the store's crammed shelves. Instead, she was greeted by the very unwelcome sight of Taryn, her nemesis from the boutique next door.

Taryn swirled on her spindly heels at the sound of Lacey's footsteps. Her dark brown pixie cut was slicked with so much gel not even a single hair moved out of place. Despite the bright June sunshine, she was dressed in her signature LBD, and it showed off every sharp angle of her bony fashionista figure.

"Do you usually leave your customers unsupervised and without assistance for that long?" Taryn asked, haughtily.

From beside Lacey came the sound of a low grumble from Chester. The English Shepherd didn't care for the snooty shopkeeper at all. Neither did Gina, who emitted her own grumble before busying herself with some paperwork.

"Good morning, Taryn," Lacey said, forcing herself into a cordial disposition. "How can I help you on this beautiful day?"

Taryn flashed her narrowed eyes at Chester, then folded her arms and pinned her hawk-like gaze on Lacey.

"I already told you," she snapped. "I'm a customer."

"You?" Lacey retorted too quickly to hide her disbelief.

"Yes, *actually*," Taryn replied dryly. "I need one of those Edison lamp thingies. You know the ones. Ugly things with big bulbs on bronze stands? You always have them displayed in your window."

She started peering around her. With her thin nose held up to the air, she reminded Lacey of a bird.

Lacey couldn't help but be suspicious. Taryn's store was sleek and simplistic, with overhead spotlights that beamed clinically white light over everything. What did she want a rustic lamp for?

"Are you re-styling the boutique?" Lacey asked gingerly, coming out from behind the desk and gesturing for Taryn to follow her.

"I just want to inject a bit of character into the place," the woman said as her heels clicked behind Lacey. "And as far as I can tell, those lamps are very *in* at the moment. I'm seeing them everywhere. At the hairdresser's. In the coffeeshop. There were about a million of the things in Brooke's tearoom..."

Lacey froze. Her heart began thumping.

Just the mention of her old friend's name filled her with panic. It had barely been a month since her Australian friend had chased after her wielding a knife, trying to silence Lacey after she'd worked out she'd killed an American tourist. Lacey's bruises had healed, but the mental scars were still fresh.

So that's why Taryn was asking for an Edison lamp? Not because she wanted one, but so she had an excuse to bring up Brooke's name and upset Lacey! She really was a nasty piece of work.

Losing all enthusiasm to help Taryn, even if she was a supposed customer, Lacey pointed limply over to "Steampunk Corner," the section of the store where her collection of bronze lamps lived.

"Over there," she muttered.

She watched Taryn's expression turn sour as she scanned the array of aviator goggles and walking canes, and the full-sized aquanaut's suit. To be fair to her, Lacey wasn't that keen on the aesthetic either. But there was a whole bunch of individuals in Wilfordshire—the type with long black hair and velvet capes—who visited her store regularly, so she sourced the items specifically for them. The only problem was, the new section blocked her previously unspoiled view across the street to Tom's patisserie, which meant Lacey could no longer dreamily gaze out at him whenever the mood struck her.

With Taryn occupied, Lacey took the opportunity now to glance across the street.

Tom's store was as busy as ever. Busier, even, with the increased amount of tourists. Lacey could make out his six-foot-three figure darting around, working at hyperspeed to fulfill everyone's orders. The light streaming in from the June sunshine made his skin look even more golden.

Just then, Lacey caught sight of Tom's new assistant, Lucia. He'd employed the young woman just a few weeks ago so that he would have more free time to spend with Lacey. But ever since the girl had started working there, the patisserie had been busier than ever!

Lacey watched on as Lucia and Tom almost bumped into one another, then both took a step right, another left, attempting to avoid a collision but ending up in comical synchronization. The slapstick routine ended with Tom theatrically bowing, so Lucia could pass on his left. He flashed her one of his bright-kilowatt smiles as she did.

Lacey's stomach clenched at the sight of them. She couldn't help it. Jealousy. Suspicion. These were all new emotions for Lacey, ones she seemed to have only acquired since her divorce, as if her ex-husband had slipped them within the pages of their divorce documents in order to make sure her future relationships were as fraught as possible. They were ugly feelings, but she couldn't control them. Lucia got to spend significantly more time with Tom than she did. And the time she spent with him was when he was at his best—energized, creative, and productive, rather than snoozily watching television on her couch. Everything felt unbalanced, as if they were sharing Tom and the ratios were massively skewed in the young woman's favor.

"Pretty, isn't she?" came Taryn's voice in Lacey's ear, like the devil on her shoulder.

Lacey bristled. Taryn was just stirring the pot as usual.

"Verrrrry pretty," Taryn added. "It must drive you mad to know Tom's over there all day with her."

"Don't be stupid," Lacey snapped.

But Taryn's appraisal was, to use a Gina idiom, "bang on." That is to say, she was totally right. And that just made Lacey more frustrated.

Taryn smiled thinly. A malevolent sparkle appeared behind her eyes. "I keep meaning to ask. How is your Spanish man? Xavier, wasn't it?"

Lacey bristled even more. "He's not my Spanish man!"

But before they could enter into a spat, the doorbell tinkled noisily, and Chester began to yip.

Saved by the bell, Lacey thought, hurrying away from Taryn and her snakelike suggestions.

But when she saw who was waiting, she wondered if it was a case of out of the frying pan and into the fire.

Carol, from the B&B, was standing in the middle of the shop floor with a look of abject horror on her face. She seemed panicked, and was panting as if she'd run all the way here.

Lacey felt her stomach lurch. A horrible sense of déjà vu overcame her. Something had happened. Something bad.

"Carol?" Gina said. "What's the matter, ducky? You look like you've seen a ghost."

Carol's bottom lip began to tremble. She opened her mouth as if attempting to speak, but then closed it again.

From behind, Lacey heard the clip-clip sound of Taryn's heels as she hurried over, presumably wanting a ringside view of the unfolding drama.

The anticipation was killing Lacey. She couldn't bear it. Dread seemed to be flooding through every fiber of her body.

"What is it, Carol?" Lacey demanded. "What's happened?"

Carol shook her head vigorously. She took a deep breath. "I'm afraid I have some terrible news …"

Lacey braced herself.

CHAPTER TWO

W hat could have happened?
         An accident?
A ... *murder*?
God forbid, not another one!

"Carol?" Lacey asked, her vocal cords feeling squeezed.

The look of fear in Carol's eyes as she paced back and forth across the shop floor was sending lightning bolts of panic straight through Lacey. Her stomach started somersaulting, as if she'd driven her second-hand Volvo off the side of the cliff and was careening toward the ocean below. She felt her hands begin to tremble as a succession of memories invaded her mind: Iris's body lying on the floor of her manor house; Buck's sand-smeared mouth as he lay deceased on the beach. Then the flashing images were joined by the sudden screech of police sirens in her ears, and that awful crinkly sound of the silver blanket the paramedics wrapped around her shoulders. And finally, she heard the voice of Superintendent Turner, echoing his warning in her mind. *"Don't leave town, okay?"*

Lacey grabbed the counter to steady herself, braced for whatever awful news Carol was about to deliver. She was barely able to focus on the woman who was pacing around the shop floor.

"What is it?" Gina asked impatiently. "What's happened?"

"Yes, please hurry up and drop your bombshell," Taryn said, lazily, waving the Edison lamp carelessly as she spoke. "Some of us have lives to get back to."

Carol finally stopped pacing. She turned to face the three of them, her eyes rimmed with red.

"There's..." she began, snuffling on her words. "A...a...a *B&B* opening!"

A beat of silence passed as the three women let the revelation—or lack of one—sink in.

"Ha!" Taryn finally exclaimed. She slapped a twenty-pound note down on the counter beside Lacey. "I'll leave you to deal with this crisis. Thanks for the lamp."

And with that, she waltzed away, leaving a scent of smoky cedar perfume in her wake.

Once she was gone, Lacey turned her attention back to Carol, staring at her in disbelief. Of course, a new B&B was terrible news for *Carol*, who would be facing even stiffer competition for the tourist trade than she already did, but it didn't make one jot of difference to Lacey! And considering the awful misfortune the town had experienced with the murder of Iris Archer and the more recent murder of Buck, she ought to know better than to run around town screaming over something so trivial!

All Lacey seemed able to do was blink. Her fury seemed to have routed her tongue well and truly to her palate. Gina's tongue, on the other hand, was as loose as ever.

"That's *it*?" she bellowed. "A B&B? You nearly gave me a bloody heart attack!"

"A B&B in Wilfordshire is terrible news for everyone," Carol cried again, frowning at Gina's response. "Not just me!"

"Really?" Lacey said, finally finding her voice. "And why would that be exactly?"

Carol shot her a daggered look. "Huh, well I should've known you wouldn't understand. You are an outsider, after all."

Lacey felt herself flame with rage. How dare Carol call her an outsider? She'd been here for several months, and had contributed to the local town in a myriad of ways! Her store was as much a part of the fabric of the high street as anyone else's.

She opened her mouth to respond, but before she did, Gina snatched up a box of tissues from the counter and stepped forward, creating a physical barrier between her and Carol.

"Why don't you take a seat?" Gina said to the B&B owner. "Let's talk all this through." Then she flashed Lacey a look that said, *I'll handle this, because you're about to blow.*

She was right. The panic Carol's non-event had induced in Lacey was starting to subside, but she really could've done without it in the first place. And she certainly could've done without Carol calling her an outsider! If anything could rile Lacey, that was it.

As Gina guided Carol to a red leather loveseat, offering her a tissue—"Here. Take one of these for your snoz"—Lacey paced away and took several calming breaths. As she did, Chester looked up at her and let out a sympathetic whinny.

"I'm all right, boy," she told him. "Just a bit rattled." She bent down and patted his head. "I'm okay now."

Chester whined as if in reluctant acceptance.

Bolstered by his support, Lacey went over to the loveseat to find out what was really going on.

Carol was full on sobbing now. Gina slowly rolled her eyes up until her deadpan expression locked with Lacey's. Lacey made a shooing gesture with her hand. Gina quickly vacated her seat.

Lacey perched beside Carol, the design of the loveseat forcing her to sit thigh to thigh with the woman; far closer than Lacey would ever choose if not for the circumstances.

"It's that bloody new mayor's fault," Carol wailed. "I knew he was trouble!"

"The new mayor?" Lacey said. She didn't know anything about there being a new mayor.

Carol turned her angry red eyes to Lacey. "He's had the east half of town rezoned. That whole area beyond the canoe club's been changed from residential to commercial! He's going to have a shopping mall built! Filled with horrible, characterless chain stores!" Her voice grew more and more incredulous. "He wants to build a *water park*! Here! In Wilfordshire! Where it rains for two-thirds of the year! And then he's going to build this monstrosity of a viewing tower! It'll be such an eyesore!"

Lacey listened to Carol's ranting, though she failed to understand why this was such a big problem. As things stood at the moment, barely anyone ventured beyond the canoe club. It was pretty much dead space. Even the beach on that side of town was rugged. Developing the area seemed like a good idea to her, especially if there was going to be a high-class B&B to service it all. And surely that would benefit all the businesses on the high street, with the increased tourism.

Lacey looked up at Gina to see if her expression might hold any clues as to why this was supposedly such a big crisis. Instead, Gina was barely hiding the smirk on her face. Clearly, she thought Carol was being over-dramatic, and if *Gina* thought you were being overdramatic, then you really had problems!

"She's some go-getter from *London*," Carol continued ranting. "Twenty-two years old. Fresh out of uni!"

She took another tissue from the box and blew her nose noisily, before handing the soggy scrunched thing back to Gina. The smirk was immediately wiped from Gina's face.

"How does a twenty-two-year-old open a B&B?" Lacey said, her tone one of marvel rather than Carol's disdain.

"By having rich parents, obviously," Carol sneered. "Her parents owned that huge retirement home in the hills. You know the one?"

Lacey could just about bring it to her memory, though she'd barely ventured that way. From what she remembered, it was a very large estate. It would require an enormous renovation to turn it from a dated retirement home to a B&B, not to mention some development of the infrastructure. It was a good fifteen-minute walk out of town and there were only two buses an hour that served that part of the coast. It seemed like a lot for a twenty-two-year-old to take on.

"Anyway," Carol continued. "The parents decided to retire early and sell off their retirement portfolio, but each of her kids got to choose one property each to do what they wanted with. Can you *imagine* being twenty-two and being *given* a property? I had to work my fingers to the bone to start my business and now Little Miss Thing is just going to waltz in and start hers like that." She snapped her fingers aggressively.

"We should count ourselves lucky she decided on something as sensible as a B&B," Gina said. "If I'd been given a huge house at her age, I'd probably have opened a twenty-four-hour nightclub."

Lacey couldn't help herself. She let out a bark of laughter. But Carol dissolved into tears.

Just then, Chester decided to come over and see what all the commotion was about. He rested his head in Carol's lap.

What a sweetheart, Lacey thought.

Chester didn't know Carol was being dramatic about nothing. He just thought she was a human in distress who deserved some comfort. Lacey decided to take a page out of his book.

"Sounds to me like you're panicking over nothing," she said to Carol, softly. "Your B&B is iconic. The tourists love the Barbie-pink house on the high street just as much as they love Tom's window sculptures made from macarons. A luxury B&B can't compete with your period property. It has its own quirky style and people love it."

Lacey had to ignore the sound of sniggering coming from Gina. Quirky had been a carefully selected word to describe all the flamingos and palm ferns, and she could just imagine the different ones Gina would've chosen: gaudy, tacky, garish...

Carol looked up at Lacey with watery eyes. "You really think so?"

"I know so! And besides, you have something Little Miss Thing doesn't. Grit. Determination. Passion. No one handed you the B&B on a plate, did they? And what kind of Londoner really wants to settle down in Wilfordshire at the ripe old age of twenty-two? My bet is Little Miss Thing will get bored soon enough and go off to greener pastures."

"Or grayer pastures," Gina quipped. "You know, because of all the roads in London? That she'll be going back to... oh, never mind."

Carol collected herself. "Thank you, Lacey. You really made me feel better." She stood and patted Chester on the head. "You too, darling dog." She dabbed her cheeks with her tissue. "Now, I'd better get back to work."

She tipped up her chin and left without another word.

As soon as the door closed behind her, Gina started laughing.

"Honestly," she exclaimed. "Someone needs to give that woman a reality check! She's really in the wrong business if she thinks a twenty-two-year-old novice is a threat. You and I both know this London kid will be out of here as soon as she's got enough money together to buy a warehouse apartment in Chelsea." She shook her head. "I think I'll take my break now, if you don't mind? I've had quite enough excitement."

"Go for it," Lacey said, just as the door tinkled to usher in another customer. "I've got this."

Gina patted her knees to get Chester's attention. "Come on, boy, walkies."

He leapt up and the two headed for the door. The short, slim young woman who'd just entered took a wide step to the left, in that tell-tale way of a person who was scared of dogs and expecting them to jump up and bite them.

Gina gave her a curt nod. She didn't have much time for people who didn't like pets.

Once the door had closed behind Gina and Chester, the girl seemed to relax. She approached Lacey, her patchwork skirt swishing as she went. Paired with an oversized knitted cardigan, her outfit wouldn't look out of place hanging in Gina's closet.

"Can I help you?" Lacey asked the woman.

"Yes," the young woman said. She had a timid energy about her, her mousy brown hair that lay unstyled over her shoulders adding to her childlike air, and her large eyes giving her something of a rabbit-in-the-headlights look. "You're Lacey, right?"

"That's right."

It never failed to make Lacey feel disconcerted when people knew her by name. Especially considering what had happened with Brooke...

"I'm Suzy," the girl said, holding out her hand to shake Lacey's. "I'm opening a B&B along the coast. Someone gave me your name as a good contact for furniture."

Lacey wished Gina was still here so she could exchange a surprised look with her, but alas she was alone, and so she shook the hand being proffered to her. She couldn't quite believe this tiny slip of a girl was the rich London graduate who had struck such fear into Carol. She barely looked over sixteen, and was as timid as a mouse. She looked like she was on her way to church, not about to open a business.

"What is it that you're looking for?" Lacey asked, masking her surprise with politeness.

The girl shrugged bashfully. "I'm not really sure yet, to be honest. All I know is that I don't want anything modern. The estate is far too big for modern. It would feel corporate and soulless, you know? It needs to feel cozy. Luxurious. Unique."

"Well, why don't we walk around the store and see if we can get some inspiration?" Lacey said.

"That's a great idea!" Suzy replied, grinning a youthful smile of exuberance.

Lacey led her to Steampunk Corner. "I was an interior designer's assistant for about fourteen years back in New York," she explained as Suzy began perusing the shelves. "You'll be amazed at where you can draw inspiration from."

Suzy was peering curiously at the aquanaut's suit. Lacey had a sudden vision of a steampunk-themed B&B.

"Let's go this way," she said hurriedly, diverting Suzy's attention toward the Nordic Nook instead.

But nothing in her Scandinavian-inspired section seemed to spark excitement in Suzy, so they continued weaving through the store. Lacey had really built up quite the collection of items during her short months as an antiquarian.

They walked the length of Lamp Lane before ending in Vintage Valley.

"Seen anything that catches your eye?" Lacey asked.

Suzy twisted her lips as if uncertain. "Not really. But I'm sure you'll be able to find something."

Lacey hesitated. She thought the whole purpose of the shop tour was to find something *Suzy* felt inspired by, not her!

"I'm sorry," Lacey said, a little perplexed. "What do you mean?"

The young woman was busy rummaging in her cloth purse and evidently didn't hear her. She pulled out a diary, thumbing through the pages, then clicked the top of a pen and peered eagerly at Lacey. "Are you free tomorrow?"

"Free for what?" Lacey asked, her confusion growing.

"The renovation," Suzy said. "Didn't I ...?" She trailed off and her cheeks went bright red. "Shoot. Sorry." She quickly shoved the pen and diary back into her shoulder bag. "I'm new to all this business stuff. I get things in the wrong order all the time. Let me start at the beginning. So, my plan is to get the B&B furnished in time for the air show and..."

"Let me stop you right there," Lacey interrupted. "What air show?"

"*The* air show," Suzy repeated.

From the frown that had appeared between her eyebrows, Lacey deduced it was her turn to be perplexed.

"Next Saturday?" the young woman continued. "Red Arrows? Castle of Brogain? You really don't know what I'm talking about?"

Lacey was stumped. Suzy may as well be talking another language. "You might've guessed from my accent, I'm not from around these parts."

"No, of course." Suzy blushed again. "Well, air shows are quite common here in the UK. You get shows all across the coast, but the Wilfordshire one is a special gem because of Brogain castle. The Red Arrows do a very exciting formation as they pass over it, and every high schooler studying photography wants to come and get a black-and-white shot of it. The juxtaposition of old war and new war." She printed the words in the air with her hands and giggled. "I know, because I was one of those high schoolers once."

All four years ago, Lacey thought.

"There's also about a zillion professional photographers who come as well," Suzy continued in a way that made it clear to Lacey she was a nervous rambler. "It's like a competition, everyone trying to snap THE image, the one that the tourist board will buy. And *then*, there's the people who come to show their respects to their ancestors. And all the families who just want to look at planes doing barrel rolls."

"I guess I need to brush up on my local history a little bit," Lacey said, feeling woefully ignorant.

"Oh, I'm just a history nerd, that's all," Suzy quipped. "I love thinking about how people lived a few generations back. I mean, it wasn't that long ago that people would go and shoot game for their dinner! The Victorians in particular fascinate me."

"Victorians..." Lacey repeated. "Shooting." She clicked her fingers. "I have an idea!"

Something about Suzy's wide-eyed enthusiasm had made the dusty cogs in the abandoned part of Lacey's interior designer mind grind back to life. She led Suzy into the auction room and along the corridor toward the office.

Suzy watched on with intrigue as Lacey opened up the safe and pulled out the wooden case containing the flintlock rifle, before clicking open the latches, raising the lid, and carefully removing the antique weapon.

Suzy drew in a sharp breath.

"Inspiration for your B&B," Lacey said. "Victorian hunting lodge."

"I..." Suzy stammered. "It's..."

Lacey couldn't tell if she was appalled or astonished.

"I love it!" Suzy gushed. "It's a brilliant idea! I can just see it now. Blue tartan. Velvet. Corduroy. An open fire. Wood panels." Her eyes had gone round with wonder.

"And *that's* called inspiration," Lacey told her.

"How much is it?" Suzy asked eagerly.

Lacey faltered. She had not been intending to sell the gift from Xavier. She'd just meant for it to be a creative springboard.

"It's not for sale," she said.

Suzy's bottom lip stuck out in disappointment.

Lacey then recalled Gina's accusations over Xavier. If Gina thought the rifle was too much, then what would Tom think when he found out? Maybe it would be better if she did just sell it to Suzy.

"... Yet," Lacey added, making a snap decision. "I'm waiting on some paperwork."

Suzy's face lit up. "So I can reserve it?"

"You can indeed," Lacey said, returning the smile.

"And you?" Suzy asked, with a giggle. "Can I reserve you, too? As the interior designer? Please!"

Lacey hesitated. She didn't do interior design anymore. She'd left that part of her back in New York City with Saskia. Her focus was on buying and selling antiques, learning how to auction them and building her business. She didn't have time to work for Suzy and run her own store. Sure, she could put Gina in charge, but with the increased tourist trade, leaving her to man the shop alone seemed a little unwise.

"I'm not sure," Lacey said. "I have a lot on my plate here."

Suzy touched her arm apologetically. "Of course. I understand. How about you just come by and check the place out tomorrow? See whether you'd like to take on the project once you've got a better feel for it?"

Lacey found herself nodding. After everything that had happened with Brooke, she thought she'd be more wary of letting new people in. But maybe she'd be able to heal from that whole ordeal after all. Suzy had one of those infectious personalities that was easy to get swept along by. She'd make an excellent businesswoman.

Maybe Carol was right to worry.

"I guess there's no harm in taking a look, is there?" Lacey said.

This time next week, when Lacey was looking back on this moment with Suzy with hindsight, the idiom *famous last words* would spring to mind.

CHAPTER THREE

L acey drove along the seafront in her champagne-colored Volvo, windows cranked, a gentle midday sun warming her. She was on her way to the former retirement home, soon to be Wilfordshire's newest B&B, with a surprise for Suzy in her passenger seat. Not Chester—her trusty companion had been far too content snoring in a sunbeam to be disturbed, and besides, Lacey was pretty certain Suzy was scared of dogs— but the flintlock rifle.

Lacey wasn't sure if she was doing the right thing by parting with it. When she'd held the rifle, it felt like it belonged to her, as if the universe was telling her she was supposed to take care of it. But Gina had planted a worm in her ear over Xavier and his intentions and she just couldn't see through the clouds.

"I guess it's too late now," Lacey said with a sigh. She'd already promised to sell it to Suzy, and it would look very unprofessional to back out of the sale now because of nothing more than a funny feeling!

Just then, Lacey passed Brooke's old tearoom. It was all boarded up. The refurbishment she'd done in transforming the old canoe shed into a swanky eatery had all gone to waste.

Thinking of Brooke made Lacey feel on edge, which was really the last thing she needed to add to the disquiet she already felt about parting ways with the rifle.

She pressed her pedal to the ground, speeding up in the hope she could leave those horrible feelings behind her.

Soon, Lacey reached the east side of town, the less populated area untouched by the sprawl of stores that spread from north to south and west to center, the area that, according to Carol, Mayor Fletcher was going to change for the worse.

Just then, Lacey saw the turning that led to the former Sunrise Retirement Home, and took a left turn onto it. The bumpy road sloped upward, and was lined with beech trees so tall they formed a tunnel that cut out the sunlight.

"That's not ominous at all…" Lacey said sarcastically. "Not in the slightest."

Luckily, the trees soon thinned out, and daylight reached her once more.

Lacey got her first glimpse of the house nestled into the hillsides. Her interior designer's mind switched immediately into gear as she assessed the exterior. It was a fairly modern-looking, red-brick, three-story mansion. She guessed it was a 1930s property that had been modernized over the years. The driveway and parking area were made of gray concrete—functional but unsightly. The windows of the manor had thick, plastic white frames—good for keeping out burglars, but a terrible eyesore. It would take more than a few strategically placed shrubs to make the exterior look like a Victorian hunting lodge.

Not that that was Lacey's problem to solve. She'd not made any decisions yet regarding Suzy's offer. She'd wanted to ask Tom for his advice, but he was working late fulfilling a last-minute order of rainbow-frosted cupcakes for the local YMCA's annual summer extravaganza. She'd also put a message on the thread she shared with her mom and younger sister, and had received a *"Don't work too hard"* response from the former, and an *"if she's paying good $$$ then go for it"* from the latter.

Lacey parked her car in the concrete parking lot, then headed up the steps that ran alongside a large, unsightly wheelchair ramp. The disabled access to the property—and presumably, within it—would be a huge plus. Neither Carol's B&B nor the Coach House Inn were suitable for guests with disabilities, neither having external access from the cobbled streets, and having narrow internal stairs with no elevator inside.

At the top of the steps, Lacey reached a large glass conservatory-style porch. It was so '90s it reminded her of a leisure center.

The doors swished open, and she went inside, where her eyes were assaulted by a huge expanse of linoleum, harsh strip lights overhead, and tacky waiting-room blinds hanging in each of the windows. A water cooler went *glug glug glug* in the corner beside an array of buzzing vending machines.

So Suzy had been understating just how much work there was to do.

"Lacey! Hey!" came the young woman's chipper voice.

Lacey peered around and saw her pop up from behind the reception desk—a huge, fake wood monstrosity that appeared to have been molded out of the very fabric of the building.

"I was just checking out the power socket situation back here," Suzy explained. "Greg, the events planner, needs to know how many electricity points are available. He's a total dragon, seriously. If I had more time, I'd hire someone else. But beggars can't be choosers. So Grumpy Greg it is." She grinned.

"What do you need an events planner for?" Lacey asked.

"The launch party, of course," Suzy said.

Before Lacey had a chance to ask her any more about that, Suzy came out from around the big desk and embraced her. It took her by surprise. But in spite of the fact they barely knew one another, Lacey found it felt quite natural. It was as if the young woman was an old friend, even though they'd only first met less than twenty-four hours ago.

"Can I get you a cup of tea?" Suzy asked. Then she blushed. "Sorry, you're American. You'll want coffee instead, right?"

Lacey chuckled. "I've gotten a taste for tea since moving here, actually. But I'm good, thanks." She was careful not to let her gaze trail over to the vending machine, and the watery, substandard tea it would presumably make. "Shall we do the tour?"

"Wasting no time, I like that," Suzy said. "Okay, well obviously this is the reception area." She opened her arms wide and grinned enthusiastically. "As you can probably tell, it's basically a conservatory they added on in the nineties. Beyond ripping the whole thing down, I've no idea how to make this look like a Victorian lodge, but I guess that's what your expertise is for. I mean, *if* you do decide to work for me." She giggled and gestured toward the set of internal double doors. "This way."

They entered a long, dimly lit hallway. A set of shiny plastic signs were screwed into the wall giving directions to the "TV room," "dining room," "garden," and "nurses' station." There was a very distinct smell about the place, like talcum powder.

Lacey wrinkled her nose. The reality of just how much of an undertaking this would be was becoming evident, and Lacey felt a creeping sense that it would just be too much to take on.

She followed Suzy into the TV room. It was a humongous space, sparsely furnished, and with the same fake wood linoleum on the floor. The walls were covered in textured paper.

"I'm thinking we'll turn this room into the drawing room," Suzy began, waltzing through the room, her patterned gypsy skirt flowing behind her. "I want an open fireplace. I think there's one boarded up behind this alcove. And we can put some nice rustic antique stuff over in this corner." She gestured vaguely with her arms. "Or that one. Whichever you prefer."

Lacey felt increasingly uncertain. The work Suzy wanted her to do was more than simple interior design! She didn't even have the layout down. But she seemed to be a dreamer, which Lacey couldn't help but admire. Throwing oneself into a task without any prior experience was how Lacey rolled, after all, and that risk had paid off for her. But the other side of the coin was that Lacey hadn't had anyone around to be the voice of reason. Other than her mom and Naomi—who'd been an entire ocean and five-hour time difference away—there had been no one there to tell her she was being crazy. But to actually be that person, watching someone dive into an almost impossible task headfirst... Lacey just wasn't sure she could do it. She didn't have the heart to bring someone down to earth with a bump and dash their dreams, but she also wasn't the type to stand back and watch as the ship sank.

"The dining room can be accessed through here," Suzy was saying, in an easy-breezy manner. She quickly led Lacey through to the next room. "We'll keep this room as the dining room because it has access to the kitchen through there." She pointed at a swing door to her right. "And it has the best view of the sea here, and the lawns."

Lacey couldn't help but notice that Suzy was already talking as if she was going to take the job. She bit down on her lip with trepidation and paced over to the sliding glass doors that took up the entirety of the far wall. The garden, though several acres, only contained grass and a few sporadically placed benches facing toward the ocean view in the distance.

"Gina would love this," Lacey said over her shoulder, searching for a positive.

"Gina?" Suzy asked.

"The lady who works at my store with me. Frizzy hair. Red glasses. Wellington boots. She's an amazing gardener. This would be like a blank canvas for her." She looked back at Suzy. "She tried to teach me how to garden but I think I'm still way too New York City for plant life."

Suzy laughed. "Well, when it's time to do the garden, I'll give Gina a call."

Suzy continued the speedy tour—through the kitchen, back out to the corridor, along to the elevator and up to one of the bedrooms.

"They're very well sized," Suzy told her, as she gestured Lacey inside.

"I'll say," Lacey replied, calculating just how much furniture would be required to furnish them appropriately.

They'd need more than just the usual B&B room bed, closet, and bedside tables that most rooms had. They were big enough for a separate couch and armchair area, with coffee table, and for a dressing area with a vanity stool. Lacey could picture it, but it was going to take a heck of a lot of coordination to get it all done in time for Saturday's air show.

"And how many rooms did you say there were?" she asked, peering nervously back out the door and along the dark corridor, which was lined either side with doors. She didn't want to make it quite so obvious to Suzy just how much work would need to be done to get this place up to scratch, so as she ducked back into the room, she rearranged her features into something altogether more receptive.

"There's four hundred square meters of accommodation in total," Suzy explained. "Six bedrooms and a bridal suite. But we don't have to do everything all at once. Just the drawing room, dining room, and a few of the bedrooms. Two or three would do to begin with, I think."

She sounded so relaxed about the whole thing, despite not actually knowing the exact amount of bedrooms she wanted furnished!

"And you need that all done in time for the air show on Saturday?" Lacey asked, as if seeking extra clarification would somehow make it make sense.

"Actually, Friday," Suzy corrected. "That's when I'm holding the launch party."

Lacey remembered Suzy mentioning Grumpy Greg the events planner, and the launch party, her question about when that was going to be had gotten lost in the moment when Suzy had hugged her by surprise.

"Friday..." Lacey repeated hypnotically, as she followed Suzy back out of the room and into the elevator.

The doors closed softly behind them and Suzy turned her eager eyes to Lacey. "So? What do you think?"

The elevator started its descent, making Lacey's stomach flip.

"You have quite a gem here," Lacey said, choosing her words carefully. "But the turnaround time is tight. You do know that, right?"

"That's what Grumpy Greg said," Suzy replied, her lips twisting, her tone becoming more morose. "He said organizing a full fireworks display in time for Friday would be nearly impossible."

Lacey held her tongue, although what she really wanted to say was that sourcing a bunch of fireworks was significantly less difficult than turning a four-hundred-square-meter care home into a Victorian hunting lodge with period furniture. If the events planner thought the turnaround was tight, then where did that leave her?

The elevator doors pinged open and they stepped out together into the main corridor, with its linoleum floor and myriad of signage and medical posters drilled into the walls.

Lacey caught Suzy peering at them, as if she'd only just seen them. As if it had only now occurred to her just how much work was needed to transform this place. For the first time, she looked a little overwhelmed. Worry began to shine in her eyes.

"Do you think I've bitten off more than I can chew?" she asked, as they headed back into the foyer.

Lacey's instincts to not disappoint her kicked in.

"I'm not going to lie," she said carefully. "It will be a lot of hard work. *But* I do think it's possible. I already have quite a lot of stock that would be appropriate for the theme. But there's some really big things you need to prioritize before any decorating can begin."

"Like what?" Suzy asked, grabbing a piece of scrap paper, as if hanging on Lacey's every word of expertise.

"The floors," Lacey began, pacing through the room. "This linoleum has got to go. The walls need to be stripped of that horrible textured paper. The artex ceiling. Opening up the fireplace alone will take a whole team..."

"So basically, gut the place and start again?" Suzy interrupted, looking up from her notes.

"Pretty much. And don't take shortcuts. When it comes to interiors, it's all about the small details. You need to create a fantasy. No fake wallpaper made to look like wood paneling. If you're going to go for paneling, make it real. Fake looks cheap. So sourcing that is an absolute priority."

Suzy went back to scribbling, nodding the whole time Lacey spoke. "Do you know a good handyman?"

"Suzy, you need *ten* handymen," Lacey told her. "At least! And a whole soccer team's worth of decorators. Have you even got the budget for all of this?"

Suzy looked up. "Yes. Pretty much. I mean, I won't be able to pay anyone until the hotel starts bringing in money, which might make it harder to find people to agree to do the work..."

Her voice trailed away, as she flashed Lacey a hopeful, puppy-dog look.

Lacey felt even less certain than she had before. Not being paid in advance would be risky, since she'd have to source a bunch of merchandise that would run into the tens of thousands of pounds. And taking on such a big project when the turnaround time was so tight, and when she had her own business to think about, may be unwise. But on the other hand, she'd really enjoyed the tour, and could picture how the place would look filled up with antique pieces. She'd also enjoyed accessing her old expertise over interior design, and combining it with her new talents for antiquing. Suzy was presenting her with a unique opportunity, and the B&B was absolutely certain to turn a profit very quickly, indeed. Yes, it would be a huge financial risk, and a massive drain of her time and energy, but when would Lacey get a chance like this again?

Not quite ready to give Suzy a definitive answer, Lacey said, "Hold that thought."

She went out to her car and fetched the flintlock in its case and carried it back into the estate.

"The rifle!" Suzy beamed, grinning at the sight of it. She looked just as thrilled to see it as she had the first time Lacey had shown it to her yesterday at the store. "You brought it? For me?"

"Yup," Lacey told her.

She placed it on the reception desk and clicked open the latches.

Suzy reached in and took it out, running her fingers over the barrel lovingly. "Can I pick it up?"

"Sure," Lacey said.

Suzy lifted it and adopted a shooting stance. She looked like something of a pro, so much so that Lacey was about to ask her if she'd ever been hunting herself. But before she got the chance, there came the sound of the automatic foyer doors swishing open behind them.

Lacey turned to see a man in a dark suit striding in through the doors. Following behind him was a woman in a presidential-looking dark crimson skirt-suit. Lacey recognized the woman from town meetings. It was Councilor Muir, their local MP.

Suzy swirled too, rifle still in hand.

At the sight of it, the man in the suit barreled into Councilor Muir protectively.

"Suzy!" Lacey squealed. "Put the rifle down!"

"Oh!" Suzy said, her cheeks flaming red.

"It's just an antique!" Lacey told the security man, who was still protectively huddling his arms around Councilor Muir.

Finally, a little hesitantly, he released her.

The councilwoman straightened out her suit and patted down her hair. "Thank you, Benson," she said stiffly to the aide who'd been about to take a bullet for her. She looked embarrassed more than anything.

"Sorry, Joanie," Suzy said. "For pointing a gun in your face."

Joanie? Lacey thought. That was a very familiar way to address the woman. Did the two know one another on a personal level?

Councilor Muir said nothing. Her gaze flicked to Lacey. "Who's this?"

"This is my friend Lacey," Suzy said. "She's going to decorate the B&B. Hopefully."

Lacey stepped forward and proffered her hand to the councilor. She'd never actually seen her up close, just speaking from the town hall's podium, or on the occasional flyer that was posted through the store's letterbox. She was in her fifties, older than in her PR photo; the lines around her eyes gave her away. She looked tired and stressed, and didn't take Lacey's outstretched hand, since her arms were full cradling a thick manila envelope.

"Is that my business license?" Suzy squealed with excitement as she noticed it.

"Yes," Councilor Muir said hurriedly, shoving it toward her. "I was just coming by to drop it off."

"Joanie sorted this all out for me so quickly," Suzy said to Lacey. "What's the word? You expediated it?"

"Expedited," one of the aides piped up, earning himself a sharp glare from Councilor Muir.

Lacey frowned. It was highly unusual for a councilor to be hand delivering business licenses. When Lacey had applied for her own, it had involved lots of online form-filling and sitting around in dingy council buildings waiting for the number on her ticket to be called, as if she were in the queue at the butcher's. She wondered why Suzy would get the red carpet treatment. And why were they already on first-name terms?

"Do you two know each other from somewhere?" Lacey asked, venturing to find out what the deal was here.

Suzy chuckled. "Joan's my aunt."

"Ah," Lacey said.

That made perfect sense. Councilor Muir had approved the rush job of switching a retirement home into a B&B because she had a family connection to Suzy. Carol had been right. There was a lot of nepotism at play here.

"Ex-aunt," Councilor Muir corrected, defensively. "And not by blood. Suzy is my ex-husband's niece. And that didn't play any part in the decision to grant the license. It's just about high time Wilfordshire got a decent-sized B&B. Tourism is going up year on year, and our current facilities just can't keep up with demand."

It was evident to Lacey that Councilor Muir was attempting to divert the conversation away from the obvious preferential treatment Suzy had been given. But it really wasn't necessary. It didn't change Lacey's opinion of Suzy, since it wasn't her fault she was well connected, and as far as Lacey was concerned, it showed good character that she was using her connections to do something rather than just rest on her laurels. If anyone came off looking bad, it was Councilor Muir herself, and not because she'd used her influential position to grant a huge favor to her ex-husband's niece, but because she was being so shady and evasive about it. No wonder the Carols of Wilfordshire were so opposed to the eastern regeneration project!

The crimson-clad councilor was still spouting her excuses. "The town actually has enough demand for two B&Bs this size, especially when you factor in all the extra trade we'll get from luring back the old shooting club."

Lacey was immediately interested. She thought of Xavier's note and his suggestion that her father came to Wilfordshire in the summers to shoot.

"The old shooting club?" she asked.

"Yes, the one up at Penrose Manor," Councilor Muir explained, gesturing with her arm in a general westerly direction where the estate was nestled on the other side of the valley.

"There was a forest there once, right?" Suzy chimed in. "I heard Henry the Eighth had the hunting lodge built so he could come and hunt wild boar!"

"That's right," the councilor said with a businesslike nod. "But the forest was eventually cut down. As with many English estates, the nobles took up shooting game birds once guns were invented, and that turned into the industry as we know it now. These days breeders rear mallards, partridges, and pheasants just for shooting."

"What about rabbits and pigeons?" Lacey offered, recalling the contents of Xavier's letter.

"They can be shot all year round," Councilor Muir confirmed. "The Wilfordshire shooting club taught amateurs during the off-season, and they practiced on pigeons and rabbits. Not exactly glamorous, but you have to start somewhere."

Lacey let the information percolate in her mind. It corresponded so accurately with what Xavier had said in the letter, she couldn't help but believe that her father really had come to Wilfordshire in the summers to shoot at Penrose Manor. Coupling that with the photo she'd seen of her father and Iris Archer, the former owner, and it seemed even more likely.

Was that why the gun had felt so familiar to her, because somewhere in the back of her mind she had memories she'd not been able to access?

"I never knew there was a hunting lodge at Penrose Manor," she said. "When did the shooting club stop operating there?"

"About a decade ago," Councilor Muir replied. She had a weary tone, like she would prefer not to be having this conversation. "They ceased operations because of..." She paused, evidently searching for the most diplomatic words. "... Financial mismanagement."

Lacey couldn't be certain, but there seemed to be an air of melancholy about the councilor, as if she had some kind of personal connection to the shooting club and its demise a decade earlier. Lacey wanted to ask more, to find out whether there may be more clues that led back to her father, but the conversation had swiftly moved on, with Suzy's enthusiastic, "So you see how much untapped potential there is here, and why you should totally get on board with the project!"

The councilor nodded in her stiff manner. "If you're being given a chance to get involved in the easterly regeneration of Wilfordshire," she said, "I would most certainly take it. The B&B is just the beginning. Mayor Fletcher has some very big plans for this town. If you make a name for yourself, you'll be at the top of everyone's contacts when it comes to future projects."

Lacey certainly was becoming more and more intrigued by the job offer. Not just for the huge potential to get her name out there—potentially earning a handsome profit while she was at it—but because of how connected it made her feel with Wilfordshire, and her father in turn. She wondered whether her father had seen all the potential in the town back in the days when he'd visited. Perhaps that was why he'd come here in the first place, because he saw a business opportunity and wanted to invest?

Or because he wanted to run away from his marriage and family and settle down in a place more suited to him, Lacey thought.

"Now, I must be going," Councilwoman Muir said, beckoning her entourage. They leapt immediately to attention. "I have a surgery to attend. The locals are furious about the proposed pedestrianization of the high street. Honestly, you'd think I'd approved to have lava poured into the roads the way they're acting." She gave Suzy a quick, efficient nod, then left.

As soon as she was gone, Suzy turned to Lacey with an eager look on her face, the manila envelope containing her business license now clutched in her hands.

"So?" she asked. "What do you say? Want in?"

"Can I have a bit of time to make up my mind?"

"Sure." Suzy chuckled. "We open in a week. Take up as much of that time deciding as you want."

⚜ ⚜ ⚜

Lacey opened the door to the antiques store. Boudica and Chester came bounding over to greet her. She ruffled their heads in turn.

"You're back," Gina said, looking up from the gardening magazine she'd been perusing. "How did it go with wunderkind?"

"It was interesting," Lacey said. She came over and took a stool at the desk beside her. "It's an amazing place, with a lot of potential. And the councilwoman seems to think so as well."

Gina folded her gardening magazine closed. "Councilwoman?"

"Yes, Councilor Muir," Lacey told her. "She's Suzy's aunt. This whole B&B thing seems to be part of Mayor Fletcher's plans to regenerate east Wilfordshire. Not that that's Suzy's fault, per se, but it does make her seem even more out of her depth. Who knows what her actual business plan looks like, or if it was just approved because of her aunt."

Gina tapped her chin. "Hmm. So Carol was onto something after all."

"In a way."

"But putting all that political stuff aside," Gina added, swiveling in her stool so she was directly facing Lacey. "What would it mean for *you* to get involved?"

Lacey paused. A small flicker of excitement ignited in her stomach. If she put all the nagging doubts to one side, it really was an amazing opportunity.

"It means I'd have responsibility for furnishing a four-hundred-square-meter property with period pieces. For an antique lover, that's basically heaven."

"And the money?" Gina asked.

"Oh, it'd bring in a *lot* of dollars. We're talking thousands of pounds of inventory. A whole dining room. A foyer. A bar. Six bedrooms and a bridal suite. It's a massive undertaking. Add to that the potential for more work in the future by getting my name out there, and the fact that having a B&B for special occasions like the air show will have a positive knock-on effect for the rest of the town ..."

Gina was starting to smile. "It sounds to me like you've talked yourself into it."

Lacey gave a noncommittal nod. "Maybe I have. But wouldn't it be crazy? I mean, she wants it done in time for the air show. Which is on Saturday!"

"And since when did working hard scare you?" Gina asked sassily. She gestured with her arms to the antiques store. "Look at everything you've already achieved from working hard."

Lacey was too modest to take the compliment, but the sentiment she could get behind. She'd become a risk taker. If she'd not quit her job in New York City and gotten the first flight to England, she'd never have built this wonderful life for herself. She'd be a miserable divorcee, still fetching coffee for Saskia like an intern rather than an assistant with fourteen years' experience. Taking on this work with Suzy was the sort of thing Saskia would fight tooth and manicured nail for. That alone was reason to do it.

"I think you know what to do," Gina said. She picked up the telephone and plonked it in front of Lacey. "Give Suzy a call and tell her you're on board."

Lacey stared at the phone, biting her bottom lip. "But what about all the costs?" she said. "That much inventory in such a short space of time will be a massive outgoing all at once. Way more than I'd ever usually spend on stock."

"You'll get paid for it, though?" Gina said.

"Only after the B&B starts making money."

"Which is a given, isn't it? So you're set to profit in time." Gina nudged the telephone toward Lacey. "I think you're looking for excuses."

She was right, but that didn't stop Lacey from finding another.

"What about you?" she said. "You'd have to mind the shop for a whole week? I won't have time to do anything else."

"I can run the store perfectly fine on my own," Gina assured her.

"And Chester? He'd have to stay with you while I worked. Suzy doesn't like dogs."

"I think I can handle Chester, don't you?"

Lacey looked from Gina to the phone and back again. Then, in one quick movement, she reached out, snatched up the receiver, and punched Suzy's number in.

"Suzy?" she said the second the call was answered. "I've made my decision. I'm in."

CHAPTER FOUR

"Oh, Percy, they're wonderful!" Lacey gushed down the phone, looking at the opened box filled with silver forks she'd just received from her favorite Mayfair antiques dealer. She was in the cramped back office at the store, surrounded by binders full of checklists, sketches, mood boards, detail drawings, and a whole bunch of coffee-stained mugs.

"They're all bundled into complete sets," Percy explained. "Salad, soup, fish, dinner, dessert, and oyster."

Lacey smiled broadly. "I don't know if Suzy's even planning to serve oysters, but if the Victorians had oyster forks on their tables, then we'd better have them on ours."

She heard Percy's grandfatherly chuckle through the speaker. "It does sound ever so exciting," he said. "I must say it's not often I receive an order for *anything you own that's Victorian.*"

"Yes, well," Lacey said. "I'm sure it's not often that one of your buyers is tasked with turning a retirement home into a Victorian-themed B&B in a week!"

"Tell me, are you getting any sleep?"

"A solid four hours a night," Lacey quipped.

Despite how hard she'd been working, she'd found the whole project thrilling so far. Exhilarating, even. It was like a mystery only she could solve, with a clock ticking away in the corner.

"Don't run yourself into the ground," Percy said, ever the gentle soul.

She ended the call, grabbed a marker pen, and put a large tick beside "utensils." She was halfway through her list now, having pulled about a hundred favors, driven cross-country to Bristol and Bath to collect some particularly exceptional pieces, then *out* of country to Cardiff just for a gorgeous stone water feature that would look perfect in the foyer.

The foyer had proved the most difficult to design of all the rooms. Its architecture was basically a conservatory. Lacey had taken her inspiration from Victorian structures like Alexandra Palace in London and the greenhouses of Kew Gardens. Suzy had the decorators in there right now, ripping up that lino flooring, chucking out the dentist's waiting-room blinds, and coating the white plastic frame with thin sheets of pliable metal, painted black to look like iron.

So far, the work had been fun, even with the sleep deprivation and long drives. But the dent to her bank balance was a little alarming. Lacey had collected thousands upon thousands of pounds' worth of furniture, all perfect to fit with Suzy's hunting lodge theme. And while she knew Suzy would settle the bill as soon as she'd made the money back, it still made her very uncomfortable to see the massive dip in her account. Especially considering the deal she'd made with Ivan over the mortgage at Crag Cottage. She'd hate to default on any payments to the sweet man who'd sold her her dream home, but if Suzy's bill wasn't settled by the end of June, she'd be forced to do just that.

The rifle alone was worth £5,000! Lacey had almost choked on her cappuccino when she'd researched its value in order to add it to Suzy's bill, and had immediately messaged Xavier suggesting she wire him some money. But he responded with, *it is a gift,* which made her feel bad for having immediately sold it. But not too bad. Because what man innocently sends a valuable antique to a woman without having certain thoughts on his mind? Lacey was starting to accept that Gina might have been correct about Xavier's intentions, and decided it was best to minimize her contact with him. Besides, she had a whole new lead to pursue in the search for her father now, with Penrose Manor's former shooting club, so Xavier wasn't the lifeline he'd once been.

In the main part of the store, Lacey could hear Gina bustling around. So far, the older woman had kept up with the demands of her new schedule pretty well. Her veto on heavy lifting had been temporarily suspended, and though Gina didn't mind, Lacey worried about making a pensioner work so hard.

Just then, Lacey heard the bell go in the other room, and it was followed by the soft happy *yips* of Chester and Boudica. Lacey knew immediately that that meant Tom had arrived. She stopped what she was doing and hurried to the main shop floor.

Sure enough, her beau was there, feeding his special carob treats to the dogs. He looked up at the sound of her and flashed her one of his gorgeous smiles.

It felt like eons since Lacey had last seen or spoken to him. He'd been too busy making rainbow cupcakes, and she'd been elbow deep in Victorian antiques. Between the two of them, they'd not even had a spare moment to send a text, let alone be in the same place at the same time!

Lacey rushed toward him and gave him a peck on the lips.

"My dear," she gushed. "It's been so long. What are you doing here?"

"It's Thursday," he said simply. "Lunch date day."

With their busy schedules, they'd agreed to pause their daily elevenses and scale back to a slightly more manageable weekly lunch on Thursdays. But that plan had been made before they'd both taken on their last-minute contracts, and Lacey had just assumed it would be off the cards for both of them. She'd promptly allowed it to be pushed out of her mind by the long laundry list of Victorian wares she had to source.

"Did you forget?" Tom asked.

"I wouldn't say forget exactly," Lacey said. "It's just we're both so busy..."

"Oh," Tom said, the disappointment in his voice quite evident. "You're canceling."

Lacey felt awful. She'd not even realized she had anything to cancel in the first place. But she shouldn't have assumed Tom would just shove their plans entirely away. Apparently, only she was callous enough to do that.

"I'm really sorry," Lacey said, taking his hand and giving it a playful tug. "You know we're having the grand opening of the Lodge tomorrow. I'm literally working flat out for the next twenty-four hours to get it all done. I probably won't even have time to go to sleep tonight, so I can hardly spare an hour for lunch." She chewed her lip, filled with guilt.

Tom seemed to be averting his eyes. She'd obviously really hurt his feelings.

"It's one lunch," Lacey promised him. "I just have this final hurdle. Then after the party tomorrow evening, I'll be back to a normal schedule. And you'll have finished with the cupcake bonanza, or whatever it's called…"

"…Extravaganza," Tom mumbled.

"Right. That." Lacey swung his hands back and forth, trying to keep her tone light and breezy. "Then we'll be back to normal. Okay?"

At last, Tom nodded. She had not seen him look this dejected before. In a way, it was kind of heartening, especially considering how worried she'd let herself get over Lucia. Turned out a very good antidote for jealousy was being so sleep deprived she was practically an automaton.

"Hey, you know what? You should come to the party," Lacey said. She felt bad she hadn't thought to invite him before. It was supposed to be a grand opening after all, with fireworks and food, and distinguished guests and all.

"Me?" Tom said. "I don't think a pastry chef is highbrow enough for the Lodge."

"Nonsense," Lacey said. "Besides, I've never seen you in a tux, and I bet you look fabulous."

She saw a mischievous glint return to Tom's eye, reminding her of the Tom she knew and loved, rather than this sullen, disgruntled one.

"Well, as long as Suzy doesn't mind," he said. "But I can't have a late night. Me and Luce need to start baking at six a.m. tomorrow."

"Luce?" Lacey repeated. Then it dawned on her he meant Lucia.

He'd given her a pet name? One that sounded remarkably similar to the nickname Lacey herself had asked him *not* to call her, since it had been the same one her ex-husband used: Lace.

All at once, Lacey's unsettled feeling over the young woman returned to her with the force of a gale. So much for her theory of being too tired to be jealous.

"Hey, that's an idea. I should take Luce out for lunch today!" Tom said, apparently oblivious to the slightly incredulous tone Lacey had failed to hide. "You know, as a thank you for all her hard work. We've been literally flat out since I hired her, and I've had to really throw her in at the deep end. It's been quite the learning curve and she's taken it all in her stride. She's a pretty remarkable young woman, really."

Lacey felt her hands tightening into fists as she listened to Tom gush about the woman he'd just decided to take to lunch in her place. A myriad of emotions swirled around in her gut. Disappointment, of course, because she was missing out on spending time with her favorite person. Jealousy, too, that some other person would be getting his attention instead. But it was more than that, and deeper. Her jealousy wasn't just because another *person* was getting Tom's attention, but because another *woman* was. A "pretty remarkable young woman" nonetheless, with her wrinkle-free skin, ever-optimistic personality, and glistening white, perfectly aligned teeth. Then adding on top of the jealousy came embarrassment—because what would the locals think? If they saw Tom out to lunch with a pretty young woman, how long would it take for the rumor mill to start churning? Taryn for one would have a field day!

"Who will mind the patisserie?" Lacey asked, clutching desperately at any excuse to stop it from happening. "If you and *Luce* are both out at lunch ... together."

"Paul, obviously," Tom replied, a confused frown appearing between his eyebrows.

For a moment, Lacey wondered if his frown was a sign that the ever-oblivious Tom had actually picked up on the undercurrent.

"Although he was being particularly klutzy today," Tom continued. "He mixed up the whisk and the spatula. There really is something not quite wired right with that boy."

So his frown had been about Paul's lack of common sense rather than their relationship. Of course it had. Knowing the type of character Tom was, he probably had no idea that Lacey was jealous of Lucia, nor had any inkling as to *why* she might be. But from Lacey's perspective, she found it maddening that such thoughts didn't cross Tom's mind, because it made her look like a crazy woman pointing it out.

"Probably not a good idea to leave him in charge then, is it?" Lacey said. "I mean, that's the whole point of Lucia, right? To make sure someone other than Paul can run the shop."

Tom scratched the back of his head contemplatively. "Yeah, you're probably right."

For a brief moment, Lacey felt her chest lift with relief.

"But Luce deserves a treat. And I'm sure Paul won't burn the place down in an hour!"

He laughed jovially, as if the issue had been resolved.

Lacey felt her shoulders slump. But it wasn't worth the hassle today. She didn't want to look paranoid and needy, especially when they didn't have time for a proper relationship conversation for at least another few days. Best let this one lie, and approach it later on when she had more energy.

"Well, enjoy your lunch," Lacey said, kissing him on the cheek. "I'll wave at you through the windows if I get half a chance."

Tom chuckled. He took her in his arms and gave her a long, lingering kiss. Lacey accepted it, knowing it would have to sustain her for a very long time.

She watched Tom exit through the glass doors. At the same time, the huge antiques hauling van arrived and drew to a halt outside her store. It was large, but with the amount of stuff that needed to be driven from her store to the B&B, Lacey was certain they'd have to do at least two or three trips. It was going to be a very long, very tiring day.

As the hauling men climbed down from the van and started walking toward her store, Lacey felt her cell phone vibrating in her pocket. She pulled it out and saw Suzy's name flashing at her.

She answered the call.

"Where are you?" Suzy asked.

She sounded harried. Throughout the week, her sunny exterior had started to wane. Lacey couldn't blame her. It had been a lot of work for her. She couldn't imagine how much stress the inexperienced young woman was under right now.

"I thought the furniture delivery was meant to be by midday?" Suzy added.

"The van got caught in traffic on the M5," Lacey told her. "But it just pulled up."

"Oh good," Suzy said with a loud exhale. "Because Grumpy Greg is on the grumble to end all grumbles. He says he can't do anything more without knowing where the furniture will be. He's out in the garden right now complaining about the setup for the fireworks display, because some of the power sockets are broken, and he'll have to run the extension cord from the old TV room, and it doesn't stretch far enough, and blah blah blah. He says I should've hired an electrician on day one. He's such a downer."

Luckily, Lacey hadn't had to have much contact with the notoriously bad-tempered events planner. Their roles at the B&B were quite separate, and he seemed so surly all the time she always gave him a wide berth.

He was right though; Suzy should have hired an electrician. The handymen had removed all the strip lights, but no one had been tasked with replacing them. Suzy's solution was to use lamps. "Lamps are nicer anyway," she'd said. Lacey had ordered fifty more Victorian lamps to go with the thirty or so she already had in her stock, and she still wasn't sure it would be enough.

"Suzy," Lacey assured her, "you've got this. Don't let Grumpy Greg get you down. I'll be as quick as I can, and then we can get to work. It's exciting! Today's the day everything starts to come together."

"I'll be excited when I'm holding a champagne glass at the party tomorrow," Suzy said. "I just want it done now."

"Sorry to break it to you," Lacey said. "But when you're running a business, there isn't ever really a 'done.' There's just a 'more.'"

Suzy groaned. "Any more of that and I'll give you a nickname like Grumpy Greg. How'd you feel about being Commonsense Lacey?"

Lacey chuckled. "If you're not even going to use alliteration, I'd prefer Wise Lacey. Or Sagacious Lacey."

Just then, the removal guy shoved open the door with his back and yanked in his wheeled gurney.

"I've got to go," Lacey said to Suzy. "I'll be with you in an hour."

"You'd better, Late Lacey," Suzy replied.

CHAPTER FIVE

L acey could barely heave her weary body to work on Friday. She'd spent all of Thursday helping the haulers move big, heavy wooden antique furniture into their van, then unload it all at the other end and carry it into the correct rooms. And then repeat the whole sequence two further times. That ate up all the daylight hours, leaving Lacey several of the dark ones to organize the bedrooms so they were laid out in accordance with her detail sketches. In the backdrop was the constant noise coming from decorators working feverishly to get everything done, punctuated by frequent arguments between Suzy and Grumpy Greg over the launch party. One particularly pertinent argument ended with Suzy yelling, "I do not want a picture of a Spitfire on a poster for a Victorian-themed hunting lodge!"

At some point in the early hours of the morning, Lacey had gone home and face-planted in bed beside Chester, before being awoken what felt like an hour later by the sound of her blaring alarm.

Now she was slumped at the counter at her store, head in hands, a cup of freshly brewed coffee steaming beside her. Needless to say, her head was aching, and her limbs felt like they'd been cast in plaster. But she just had one day at the store and one party to get through, and then she could sleep for the rest of her life. Or, at least, for Saturday morning; Gina had agreed to open up tomorrow *and* pick up Chester on the way so Lacey could lie in.

"There," Lacey heard Gina say.

She lifted her heavy head from her hands. Gina had stuck up the new, fresh-off-the-press poster Greg had delivered to the store first thing that morning. It showed a Spitfire, the plume of fumes forming yellow bubble writing that proclaimed, "AIR SHOW PRE-PARTY at Wilfordshire's finest new establishment, the Lodge. Fireworks. Marquee. Barbeque."

"Barbeque?!" Lacey exclaimed, grimacing. "I thought Suzy wanted this to be a high-class event. She was going to have Victorian-era canapés."

The branding was all off, and it definitely didn't seem in keeping with the Victorian shooting lodge theme. Lacey really hoped Greg was right on this one. If the pre-party didn't draw in interested future clientele, then her chances of quickly recouping her upfront costs started to dwindle.

"What even is a Victorian-era canapé?" Gina asked. "Duck paté? Mutton bites? Boiled chicken strips? Barbecue is definitely a better idea. Who doesn't love a barbecue on a warm summer evening?"

"That's not the point," Lacey argued. "I know what Suzy wanted and it wasn't that. She definitely didn't agree to the Spitfire being on the poster!"

"But more people will come if they know it's in honor of the air show. If the whole purpose of the launch party is to show off the place—to get bums in seats, as they say—then this is the way to do it!"

Lacey was too tired to ask what the heck "bums in seats" meant, let alone debate issues of taste and class with Gina. Instead, she just sank her head back onto her arms.

Just then, the shop doorbell jangled as their first customer of the day entered. She was a portly woman with a long blond braid hanging over one shoulder. She took two steps, noticed the poster, then loudly exclaimed, "Ooh, barbecue!"

Gina flashed Lacey one of her *told you so* looks and turned to the customer with a big triumphant grin on her face. "That's right. There's an air show pre-party at the Lodge this evening."

"The Lodge?" the woman repeated. "I've never heard of it."

"You know Sunrise Retirement Home? On the east side? It's been converted into a B&B. This is their launch party, to coincide with the air show tomorrow. Rumor has it Mayor Fletcher will be coming."

The woman looked impressed, and Lacey thought Gina was doing a pretty good job of stoking her interest, especially considering the rumor was coming from her and her alone.

"Maybe I'll swing by after my gran's birthday," the woman said, hastily selecting a pink, flowery teapot from the chinaware's shelf and coming up to the counter. "Nana loves pink," she said simply, placing it beside the display of Victorian toy airplanes Lacey had put beside the till in honor of the air show tomorrow. "May as well get one of these as well," the woman added, grabbing a tin Spitfire with as little consideration as she had nana's pink teapot.

Lacey rang up her purchase, ignoring Gina's attempts to catch her eye, knowing she just wanted to flash her another *see!* look.

The woman paid and left.

"I really hope we have a quiet day," Lacey said as soon as the door closed behind the woman.

"Touch wood!" Gina insisted. "Or you'll jinx us!"

But before Lacey had a chance, the door flew open again and in filed a group of noisy tourists. They were wearing hats shaped like airplanes and were being led by a guide dressed like Wing Commander Biggles.

Gina glowered at Lacey and mouthed the word "Jinxed."

⚜ ⚜ ⚜

It was hours before the store was once again free of customers. Like a balloon losing all its air, Lacey sank into her stool.

"Let me get the kettle on," she heard Gina's disembodied voice say. "You need some caffeine."

"Thank you," Lacey murmured from between her arms. She had no idea how she was going to get through the day, let alone the party this evening. As much as she wanted to celebrate all her hard work, she would happily exchange a party for an early night in bed! But then she remembered it would be her first time having anything resembling downtime with Tom in ages. That, more so than the fireworks and free champagne, was a reason to go.

As Gina headed to the kitchen to brew the coffee, Lacey let her eyes flutter closed. But even then, she could still see William Morris patterns swirling on the inside of her eyelids.

Suddenly, a noise from the other side of the counter made Lacey jolt upright. To her surprise, Carol was standing over her, arms folded, glaring. Lacey hadn't even heard the bell go; she must have briefly nodded off, right there at the desk!

"Carol," Lacey said, wiping the corners of her mouth in case of drool. Thankfully, there was none. "I haven't seen you in a while."

"No, you haven't," Carol replied testily. She narrowed her eyes. "Not since I told you all about a new B&B being opened in Wilfordshire as part of Mayor Fletcher's awful regeneration project that will destroy the character of our town."

"Oh. That," Lacey said, realizing that Carol must've just found out she'd been working for Suzy. She knew she really should've told Carol herself, but there'd literally been no time! Pretty much from the second Suzy had walked into her store, Lacey had been rushed off her feet working for her.

"Yes, that," Carol said, anger smoldering in her eyes. "I can't believe you would backstab me that way!"

Backstab seemed a bit much as far as Lacey was concerned, but she did feel genuine compassion for Carol. It was never her intention to hurt people's feelings, even unintentionally, even if those people were extremely sensitive and easily offended, like Carol.

"I'm really sorry," Lacey said. "I should've told you I was working with Suzy. I hope you know it wasn't personal, it was just a good business decision."

"A good business decision for yourself," Carol snapped back. "And the rest of us can go to hell? Is that what you were thinking?"

"Carol..." Lacey started. The venom was far too excessive for the sin she'd committed.

"What about Ivan?" Carol interrupted. "You may not value my friendship that much, but Ivan has been more than generous to you."

"What has Ivan got to do with any of this?" Lacey asked, genuinely perplexed that her old landlord had been brought up.

"Because of his holiday cottage business!" Carol exclaimed, as if Lacey was extremely ignorant.

"Look, I honestly don't think the new B&B will take business away from you or Ivan," Lacey said, starting to lose her patience. "You have different markets. If I thought there was any chance your livelihoods would be harmed, I would never have taken on the project."

"Ivan's already has," Carol countered. "He owned a load of land out in the east and was trying to get licenses to open a static holiday home park. The council blocked him. And now we know why. Because Mayor Fletcher wanted a swanky B&B there instead, and Councilor Muir rushed her niece into the job!"

Lacey felt awful. She'd had no idea Ivan even owned land in east Wilfordshire, or that his business plans had been scuppered by Mayor Fletcher's regeneration plans.

"I didn't realize ..." Lacey said, dumbly.

"No. Because you have no real connection to this town. To its history. Because you thought you could swoop in from New York City and line your pockets with profit, then leave us to clean up the mess!"

She turned on her heel and marched away. Which was for the best really, because Lacey was close to losing her composure. Carol was being ridiculous, taking out on Lacey what she really ought to be directing at Mayor Fletcher.

"That was brutal," came Gina's voice from behind.

Lacey turned to see her friend in the archway holding a mug of coffee in one hand and two painkillers in the outstretched palm of the other.

"You're a good friend, Gina," Lacey said.

❖   ❖   ❖

Lacey and Gina ended up working late, since there were so many more customers than normal. By the time they finally closed their doors, the wrought iron clock read half past six. That gave Lacey just thirty minutes to drive the dogs home and get herself ready for the party. There was no way she'd make it to the Lodge in time for the 7 p.m. start. The only upside was that she'd give legitimacy to the Late Lacey nickname.

"We're going to be late for the party," Lacey said fretfully to Gina. "Suzy will be so disappointed. She really wants me there on time, because her parents are skiing in Switzerland or something, and her brothers are too sour-grapes to support her."

"Well, why don't we just go straight there from here?" Gina suggested.

"We can't do that!" Lacey said. "I look a mess." Then she looked Gina up and down. "And you're in your *wellies*!"

Gina shrugged. "So? Is there a dress code? Actually, don't tell me, I don't care. If Suzy's planning on hiring me to do her garden, she'll have to get used to seeing my wellies. Besides, they're a very demure green color, and if I recall correctly, Victorian shooters would've worn boots. So if anything, I'm perfectly dressed for the occasion."

Lacey laughed. She did love Gina's confidence. "Sure. But what about me? I have bags under my eyes the size of Australia. I was going to put on some serious warpaint."

"Nonsense," Gina added. "You look as lovely as ever."

Lacey took the compliment, even though she didn't really trust Gina's opinion when it came to that sort of thing. But in her tired, slightly fragile state, she preferred a white lie from Gina over the brutal honesty she'd get from Naomi if her sister were here.

"What about Chester and Boudica, though?" Lacey asked. "You know Suzy is afraid of dogs."

Gina rolled her eyes. "It's about high time she got over that! And I'm sure she'd prefer her friend to be there on time to give her moral support with her dog rather than late without it."

"Suzy did ask me to be there before the doors open," Lacey replied. "It's a big deal for her and I'm pretty much her only friend in this town."

"There," Gina said, triumphantly. "It's settled. We'll go straight from here."

Lacey still wasn't convinced, but she found herself agreeing with Gina, if only because she knew if she got home and caught sight of her couch, she wouldn't be able to resist sitting on it, and once she was sinking into its comfy squishiness, she'd never be able to stand up again ...

"All right. I'll tell Tom to pick us up from here instead. That'll give me about five minutes to try and sort out my face."

"*I'll* call Tom," Gina said, rolling her eyes and holding her hand out, palm up, for Lacey's phone. "That way you can have six minutes."

Lacey handed over her cell phone. "You're the best."

She hurried into the bathroom to fix her makeup. Despite the extra minute Gina had gifted her, there was still no time for a night look, so she just freshened up her minimal day look, tidied her hair, and spritzed herself with perfume. Then she switched out of her flat brogues and into a pair of heels. Finally, she put on a delicate rose gold necklace. Luckily, the androgynous suits she always wore for work could be dressed up pretty quickly, for situations like this when she only had a few minutes to go from work to an event.

Lacey hurried back out.

"Tom's on his way," Gina said, handing her back her cell phone. "He'll be here in five minutes."

Lacey looked over at the wrought iron clock to check whether she'd make it in time or not. But rather than read the time, she hit on sudden inspiration.

"The clock!" she exclaimed. "It's from the Victorian era! It'll look amazing at the B&B! It might just bring the whole external facade together! It'll make the perfect gift. Come on, help me get it down. It's heavy."

She grabbed a screwdriver from the toolbox and raced over to the clock. But once there she discovered Gina had not followed her. She turned back to see her friend pouting.

"Quick!" she cried. "Before we run out of time! No pun intended."

"You can't give the clock to Suzy," Gina replied. "It's ours."

Lacey rolled her eyes. "I can get us another clock."

"Another rare, genuine Victorian workhouse one?"

"An even better one," Lacey said. "I'll splurge on a John Walker original Victorian railway station one. Okay?"

"All right," Gina said, reluctantly. She stomped over inelegantly in her wellies. "But once we've done this can you please relax? You're meant to be off the clock. Pun definitely intended."

Lacey laughed and handed Gina the screwdriver. As the older woman began loosening the screws, Lacey took hold of the clock, ready to take the weight of it once it was released.

"Ready. Here goes," Gina said.

"Oof!" Lacey's knees buckled slightly under the weight. "Why was everything the Victorians made so heavy?"

"Now, now, Lacey, what have I taught you about sounding like a local? I think what you meant to say was, 'Why was everything the Victorians made so *bloody* heavy?'"

Whether she was just delirious from lack of sleep or from the strain of holding the heavy clock, Lacey found herself laughing uncontrollably at Gina's ridiculous sense of humor.

Gina took hold of one side of the clock, and together they awkwardly hobbled to the door with it.

"Is Tom going to mind having this in his van?" Gina asked. "It's a bit oily."

"Have you ever been inside Tom's van?" Lacey quipped. "It's full of camping equipment and climbing ropes and fishing rods. He probably won't even notice it's there."

Lacey maneuvered the cumbersome clock so she was able to free a hand. She groped behind her for the door handle, and just about managed to turn it from her awkward position.

"Chester! Boudica! It's party time!"

She couldn't see over the monstrosity of the clock, but she heard the *clip clip clip* of the dogs' claws on the wooden floorboards as they galloped over, then felt them both pushing past her legs.

"All right, let's waddle," Lacey said to Gina.

They inched out of the store, Lacey walking backward, Gina forward, the clock suspended between the two of them. Once they'd cleared the threshold, they rested it down on the pavement.

"Phew!" Gina said, wiping her brow.

Lacey locked up the store, then turned back to the street and searched for any sign of Tom's van. Thanks to the busier tourist period, the streets had more cars and taxis than usual. In fact, the streets were super busy with pedestrians, and a giant clock in the middle of the pavement was something of an obstruction.

"Where is he?" Lacey said aloud, looking up and down the street.

Just then, she saw bright headlights coming from behind the row of parked cars. It looked like a van, idling.

Of course. It was so busy, there'd been nowhere outside the store for Tom to park. He'd been forced to park a few cars back.

"I think that's him up there," Lacey said, pointing.

Gina looked at the heavy clock resting beside them, then back up at Lacey with a nonplussed expression. "Bet you're having second thoughts about gifting this now, huh?"

Lacey flashed her a wry smirk.

The two women lifted up the heavy clock and resumed their waddling up the road until they reached Tom's van. Behind the windshield, Lacey saw his lovely face emerge, and his look of amused surprise at the sight of her and Gina struggling along with the clock.

When they got around the back of the van and opened up the trunk, Lacey was surprised to discover it wasn't empty. One of Tom's largest patisserie boxes was taking up half the space.

"There's a cake in here," Lacey said, surprised.

"Oh, that's mine," came a female voice from inside the car. "Do you want me to move it over?"

Lacey peered over the back seat to see Lucia turned over her shoulder looking at her.

"What are you doing here?" Lacey said far too quickly to modulate her tone into something less hostile.

She heard the driver's door open, and Tom appeared. He kissed her cheek.

"You don't mind Luce sharing the ride with us, do you?" he asked, shoving over the cake box to make room for the clock.

Lacey was too surprised to say anything. Why was she even coming in the first place?

"What's the cake for?" was all she managed.

"It's for Suzy," Lucia called from the back seat. "A sort of congratulations cake."

"She commissioned it?" Lacey asked.

"Oh no, it's a gift," Lucia said. "Suzy and I are old friends. We took riding lessons together when we were kids."

Great, Lacey thought, feeling irritation swirl inside of her. So not only was Luce working with her lover, but she was also friends with her friend?

"Wait until you see it." Tom beamed. "Luce has been working on it all day. It's a masterpiece."

"Can't wait," Lacey said through her teeth.

"Let me help you with that," Tom said, reaching for the clock.

"I've got it, thanks," Lacey replied tersely.

She and Gina tried to maneuver the clock in beside the cake—Lacey half tempted to squish it "accidentally" in the process—but there wasn't enough room.

"I'll take it in the passenger's seat," Tom said. "If you three ladies are okay in the back with the dogs?"

"Fine with me," Gina said, before Lacey even got a chance to say she'd prefer it if she got to ride up front with her partner rather than the clock.

"It might be a bit of a squeeze," Tom said, heaving open the van door. "It didn't occur to me I'd be driving two dogs and a clock as well." He chuckled.

"After you," Lacey said, willing Gina to get in first to sit next to Lucia so she didn't have to.

"Me? With this bottom?" Gina exclaimed, smacking her behind. "No, it's better if you take the middle seat."

"Luce should take it," Tom said. "She's the slimmest here."

Lacey almost shot him a death-stare.

"That's fine!" Lucia called brightly from inside. "I'm budging into the middle."

Seething, Lacey went around the back and slid in beside Lucia.

"This is going to be so much fun," Lucia said, as the van pulled away.

"Yup," Lacey replied, unconvinced.

She was already ready for the night to be over.

CHAPTER SIX

T om pulled his van into the parking lot of the Lodge. There were already several vehicles there, from the caterer's van to Grumpy Greg's vintage red Beetle, and a bunch of other vehicles that must belong to the temp staff Suzy had drafted in for the evening.

Lacey felt a tremble of nervous anticipation ripple through her. The fruits of her labor were about to be open for the whole town's critique.

She peered out through the van's window and up the steps. The outside of the building was the same, since there'd been no time for any external facade work, but with warmer yellow light rather than harsh white strip lights spilling from the foyer, it wasn't as obvious that this was a fairly new building.

Standing in the open doorway, Lacey spotted Suzy waving. Grumpy Greg stood beside her looking as surly as ever. Lacey wondered if anyone had ever told him he'd gone into the wrong line of work. Someone that miserable should not be present at happy occasions!

Lacey was the first out of the van, sliding open the side door and hopping out as Suzy trotted down the steps, her pretty cream chiffon dress floating out behind her like a fairy.

"You're here!" she exclaimed, hop-skipping in her matching ballet pumps across the parking lot toward them. "And you look so—"

Before she had a chance to finish her sentence, Chester and Boudica, with their innate doggy ability to absorb other people's excitement and surpass it with their own, came bounding out of the van and went racing toward Suzy to greet her. Watching Suzy's expression transform from joy to abhorrence in a split second was really something to behold.

"Ah!" she screamed, twisting her body away and bringing her arms crossed defensively over her midriff.

"Stop!" Lacey commanded, before the dogs could jump up and ruin Suzy's pretty dress.

Chester and Boudica stopped obediently, sitting back on their haunches. They looked back at Lacey with mournful expressions, as if to say, *We were only saying hello.*

Suzy seemed a little surprised that they'd both stopped charging at a simple command from Lacey. Her face relaxed a little, turning the expression of horror into a slightly less dramatic one of mere disgust.

"You brought the dogs," she said, trying to sound fine with it, but failing miserably.

"I'm so sorry," Lacey said. "I had to keep the store open late, and there wasn't enough time to take them home."

"It's fine," Suzy said, a strained smile appearing on her lips. She was obviously less than thrilled about them being here. "Do you mind taking them straight out to the garden? And not through the house, via the side gate. Did you bring leashes? We'll have to tie them up to the bandstand—"

"I'll keep an eye on them," came the curt voice of Gina's voice, cutting through Suzy's nervous rapid-fire questions.

Lacey turned to see the older woman's head poking out from the van, and she did not look happy. In fact, she was wearing a look of indignation that was directed straight at Suzy. Gina often had less patience for people than animals, and Suzy's suggestion the dogs be tied up in the garden on their leashes like, well, *dogs*, must have offended her.

Talk about first impressions, Lacey thought.

"Suzy, this is Gina," she said, brightly, in an attempt to salvage the introduction. "My friend, colleague, neighbor ... surrogate mother."

"Oh!" Suzy said, sounding surprised that this was the woman Lacey had been telling her about. "You're the gardener extraordinaire? It's a pleasure to meet you."

Gina emerged fully from the van and stood before Suzy in all her disheveled glory. Suzy's eyes darted fretfully down to her Wellington boots, and she blinked, the look of alarm in her eyes barely concealed.

"Ditto," was all Gina would say.

Her unfriendly demeanor made Suzy even more nervous. Gina had been as equally frosty with Brooke, Lacey recalled, as if she actively tried to find offense in order to give herself an excuse to dislike anyone else Lacey was friends with. At least with Brooke, she'd turned out to have been right in not trusting the woman, but Lacey couldn't help thinking she was being a bit too harsh on sweet little Suzy. Especially considering Gina hadn't stopped talking about her excitement to see the garden all week, and had claimed she would spend the entire evening exploring it while eating barbequed chicken!

"Gina's desperate to see the garden," Lacey said to Suzy.

"Oh good," Suzy said hurriedly. "Then you can decide whether you'd like to take on the position of chief gardener?" She smiled her anxious smile.

Lacey wondered if Suzy's anti-dog stance might be a deal breaker, but she was confident Gina would change her mind once she saw the blank canvas of the garden.

"Come on, pups," Gina said, turning her attention to Boudica and Chester. "Heel." She led the two of them away in perfect, obedient synchronicity, as if to prove a point.

With the dogs receding from her personal space, Suzy seemed to return to her happy, animated form. They were through the gate that led around to the back garden by the time Lucia was out of the van.

It was the first time Lacey had seen her in full. She looked lovely. Her chestnut brown hair, usually hidden beneath a white netted chef's hat, was lying in bouncy waves against her shoulders. She was wearing a simple off-the-rack party dress, but with her elegant, well-proportioned figure, she made it look expensive. Unlike Lacey, she'd had enough time after work to put on a full nighttime makeup look, which had transformed her slightly baby-faced cheeks into the angled cheekbones of a sophisticated woman.

"My besties are here!" Suzy gushed, pulling both women into a three-way hug.

Squished against Lucia, Lacey felt even more uncomfortably close than she had in the van, and it suddenly occurred to her that she would *never* truly get space from the girl. She worked with her beau. They shared the same friend. Lacey was doomed to be pulled into metaphorical three-way hugs with this woman for the rest of her life.

Suzy finally released them, and Lacey saw that Tom had now exited the van and was standing beside them. Her hopes of seeing him in a tux were dashed. He'd opted for a beige linen suit, which, while perfectly complementing the golden hue of his skin and being far more fitting for his personality, was a little on the crinkled side. She should've guessed Tom would be too modest for a flashy outfit.

He and Suzy exchanged pleasantries. Then Lacey remembered the clock.

"I brought you something," she said to Suzy.

"A gift?" Suzy squealed. "For me?"

Lacey nodded, and showed her the clock resting in the back of the van. "This was from a Victorian workhouse originally. I realized it would be absolutely perfect here. It's designed to be hung outside."

"I love it!" Suzy gushed.

"I got you a gift as well," Lucia said, so quickly she clipped off the end of Suzy's sentence. "Although it's not quite as impressive as Lacey's."

Lacey couldn't tell if Lucia was giving her a genuine compliment, or if she'd just jumped in to steal her thunder and divert Suzy's attention away from the clock. She watched on as Lucia bent over into the van to retrieve the patisserie cake box, displaying a perfect, peachy derriere as she did so. Lacey side-eyed Tom to see if he was looking, but he didn't appear to be.

"Ta-da!" Lucia said, swirling around and presenting the cake to Suzy.

The cake was three-tiered, each layer held up by model horses. The frosting was white, and there were raspberries all around it.

"Told you it was marvelous," Tom said to Lacey, evidently proud of his protege, although Lacey's exhausted mind tried to twist his reaction into something more than mere admiration.

"Is it white chocolate and raspberry?" Suzy asked Lucia.

The pretty assistant nodded. "Your favorite!"

"Oh, and look at the little horses!"

While Suzy cooed over each of the figurines, Lacey tried not to compare her reactions to their gifts. But she couldn't help noticing how much more touched Suzy seemed by Lucia's cake than by the antique clock. The personal significance of the cheap plastic horses obviously meant a lot to Suzy, and was impossible for Lacey to compete with. She'd not even known the two women were friends until Lucia had materialized in Tom's van like some kind of beautiful apparition sent to torment her.

Suzy beckoned for the waiters to take the cake to the kitchen for later, while Tom and another hired hand picked up the heavy iron clock between them. Then Suzy looped her arms through Lacey's and Lucia's, and they all headed up the steps toward the foyer.

"I'm so happy you're both here," she said. "My two best friends. You know, we should all go out for brunch together sometime."

"I'd love that," Lucia said. She leaned forward to look past Suzy. "I've not had a chance to get to know you, Lacey."

Lacey forced out a friendly laugh. "Yes, we've both been so busy." She left it there, leaving her lack of a direct answer floating between them.

They reached the foyer and the automatic doors swished open to let them inside.

Lacey had been concerned that the automatic doors (of which there'd been no time to replace during the renovation) might ruin the magic, but the second she was inside the foyer, she realized she'd had no reason to worry at all.

It was like stepping back in time. Far from the reception of a leisure center, it had been transformed into the tranquil garden conservatory of Lacey's sketch. Slate tiles had replaced the linoleum. The beautiful stone water fountain took pride of position in the center of the room, with the large crystal chandelier Lacey had had flown in from a Parisian arthouse hung above it, turning the light from the wall sconces into miniature rainbows. The place was filled with plants, just like the indoor garden Lacey had sketched in her detail drawing. Gone was the ugly desk, the buzzing vending machines, and the glugging water cooler. There wasn't a strip light in sight, and the dentist's waiting room blinds had been confined to the trash where they belonged.

"This has been rechristened 'The Entrance,'" Suzy announced in a grand voice.

"It's fabulous," Lacey said.

They went into the corridor, which Lacey had designed to house the new reception desk. The plan had come together quite perfectly; the huge ornamental desk unit had been installed to the right, providing a barrier between the public part of the B&B and the back rooms and kitchen. There was a row of servant's bells hanging behind it, giving the place a sense of authenticity.

"The party will be taking place in the dining room and garden," Suzy said as she walked.

"What about the TV room?" Lacey asked. "Did the stove fitter finish in time?"

When she'd left on Thursday, the chimney specialist was still working on exposing the fireplace, which had produced an inordinate volume of soot and debris throughout the week. With the room off limits, Lacey had reluctantly left her sketches and some written instructions with the decorators. Besides the bedrooms, the vast majority of her work had gone into designing the TV room. She'd enjoyed designing it the most and was eager to see the finished product, with the antique rifle now mounted above the restored fireplace.

But Suzy just tapped her nose, and Lacey wasn't sure how to interpret that. Either there was a big reveal coming, or she was trying to say the TV room was a secret, because it hadn't been finished on time and would be closed off to the partygoers. Lacey hoped it wasn't the latter, as her impatience was getting the better of her.

They followed Suzy into the dining room, and Lacey was relieved to see the wooden floorboards had been varnished in a lovely dark, glossy brown color. The flooring specialist had taken a sick day earlier in the week and had been rushing to make up the time. There'd been a whole contingency plan in place involving a Persian rug that had seen better days, and Lacey was relieved it hadn't come to that in the end.

"These look great," Lacey said, tapping her heel on the boards.

The artex ceiling had been plastered over, the horrible strip lights had been removed, and the room was now lit by a hodge-podge of standing lamps with floral fringed shades. But Lacey was disappointed to see the banquet-style walnut tables she'd had to hire a van and drive to Bristol to collect were pushed up against the walls, covered in buffet food. It made her feel a little displeased to see them arranged like that. While she accepted that it was temporary, and had been done to create enough space in the room for mingling, it still felt disrespectful toward the artistry and engineering of the pieces for them to be used as little more than picnic tables. And finger foods in a Victorian-era hunting lodge really didn't sit right with her inner pedantic designer.

At the far end of the room, the sliding glass doors had been folded fully open, creating a seamless lead through to the outside. The dogs were already bounding around, clearly enjoying their exploration.

This was Grumpy Greg's domain, the place where his and Lacey's tastes clashed, where the modern intruded upon the old. There was a marquee, fire pit, barbeque, outdoor bar—complete with posters advertising the air show—and a very unsightly fireworks display set up at the end of the huge expanse of lawn.

At least it's all contained to the garden, Lacey thought.

If any of it had encroached on her painstakingly designed interior, she would not have been happy.

Greg glanced over from where he was conferring with the wait staff he was managing that evening, gave the group a head-to toe surveil, then turned back and carried on with his meeting. Lacey was glad she'd never have to see Grumpy Greg's sour face again.

"What do you think of the garden?" Suzy called to Gina.

Gina was looking more excited than the dogs. "I love it. I can't wait to get to work."

It seemed like she'd already put their initial meeting out of her mind.

"Next week?" Suzy asked. "Once the air show is out of the way? You can sculpt and prune in whatever way you see fit."

Gina rubbed her hands with glee at the prospect, although Lacey was a little worried about giving up her assistant. But she was thrilled for Gina. Working on the garden would be a dream for her.

"Right," Suzy said, clapping her hands together. "Time for drinks!"

They went back through the dining room. Lacey was still disappointed by how it looked with the tables pushed aside, covered in tablecloths that were definitely not in keeping, and laden with modern foods rather than Victorian delicacies. And while she knew it was only temporary, having been arranged that way for the night, she still felt like Greg had gotten more of his way than Suzy would've liked.

Lacey couldn't help but feel there wasn't much to show for all her effort; other than the stone fountain and lamps, the vast majority of furniture she'd sourced had gone to the bedrooms. But what about that gorgeous walnut corner piece? And the flintlock rifle? Where was the very thing that had sparked the inspiration for the Lodge—indeed, its name—in the first place?

As they headed out into the corridor, Lacey quickly realized Suzy was leading them to the TV room. So it had been finished in time? A flutter of nervous anticipation went through her.

Suzy paused outside the dark varnished wooden door (Lacey purchased, decorator installed) and turned to face them all, her hand poised on the handle, a small smile on her lips.

"Please enter ... the drawing room!"

She pushed the door open and Lacey's jaw dropped to the floor.

This was what she'd been wanting to see!

To the left was the walnut corner piece, being used as an understated bar area, a handsome young bartender waiting behind it. The rest of the room was set up like a cozy lounge, with the high-backed William Morris print chairs beside low coffee tables, thick dark blue velvet curtains, oil paintings of Wilfordshire, and large mahogany bookcases filled with era-appropriate books.

The focal point of the room was the old fireplace. It had been exposed and reconstructed beautifully. An oblong of brown leather couches covered in blue tartan throws surrounded it, with a genuine Persian rug in the middle. And there, above the newly installed marble mantelpiece, hung the flintlock rifle.

"Suzy, it's absolutely perfect!" Lacey exclaimed.

"And it's all thanks to you," Suzy told her.

"I'm amazed you got all this done in a week," Lucia said, pacing toward the bookshelf and peering at the spines.

Tom, meanwhile, had beelined for the rifle and was inspecting it with curiosity.

"Does this work?" he asked over his shoulder to Suzy.

Right away, Lacey felt tense. She had not told Tom about Xavier's gift, Gina having made her feel more than a little wary about it.

"Yes, it functions but isn't loaded, obviously," Suzy explained. "It was the inspiration for the whole decor. Lacey's idea, of course. The moment she showed me it in the store's backroom, the idea came together."

"Wait, this was from the store?" Tom asked, turning fully to Lacey with a surprised look in his eyes. "I didn't even know you had a license to trade firearms. How long have you been hiding this beauty?"

Lacey squirmed. "Uh... well, I had to get the license in order to store Iris Archer's guns at my store."

"It's from Penrose Estate?" Tom asked, quite innocently.

Lacey scratched her neck. "No, not quite. It was sent to me from an antiques contact."

A couple of beats passed before Tom said, "Well, it's amazing," and dropped his line of questioning.

Lacey exhaled, relieved to have dodged a bullet.

The waiter came over with a silver tray loaded with an array of facet-cut crystal sherry glasses Lacey had purchased from Percy. Of course, it would've been better if they matched, but sourcing one hundred real Victorian sherry glasses within a week had been quite a tall order.

"This is a popular Victorian dessert wine," Suzy said. She lowered her voice, "Don't tell Greg. He said no one will want it, so I snuck it behind the bar without him knowing. There's a few bottles of the stuff. Free for all of you."

The glasses were filled with a pale amber liquid. Lacey was glad Gina was in the garden. She'd be sure to say aloud how much it looked remarkably like urine.

Lacey took a glass from the tray and brought it to her lips. She took a small sip. It tasted significantly better than it looked, like a very syrupy, sickly sweet dessert wine.

"You've thought of everything," Lucia said to Suzy, but her face pinched in disgust. She must've taken a glug of the wine rather than a sip, as it was intended to be consumed.

Just then, they heard the sound of voices coming from the foyer.

"Guests!" Suzy said, her eyes widening with excitement. "Help yourself to canapes!" She deposited her glass and floated out of the room.

Lacey didn't need telling twice. She'd been working so hard she'd not eaten enough for days, and so she went over to the bar where the handsome bartender had laid out several more plates of finger foods.

She worked her way through the selections on offer, enjoying the juxtaposition of sweet caramelized carrot chutney and sharp, tangy cheese. Then onto the pancake blini topped with king prawn and avocado, which was even more delicious than the last. She moved on to the more savory flavor combinations of pastrami with mustard, gherkin and sauerkraut on rye bread, and finished it off with a prosciutto and red pepper tapenade.

"Guys, you should try the food," she said, turning back. "It's heavenly..."

Her voice disappeared. Tom and Lucia were in a silent fit of hysterics over their sickly-sweet drinks, lost in their shared joke. The look passing between them was not lost on Lacey.

"Come on," Lacey said brusquely. "Let's get this party started."

Her mood to celebrate had been entirely vanquished.

CHAPTER SEVEN

"That's a reporter," Suzy whispered, pointing theatrically around the corridor wall into the foyer. "From the *Wilfordshire Weekly*."

"I'm not surprised," Lacey said, taking in the sight of the brown-corduroy-clad woman holding a Dictaphone. "The Lodge is the talk of the town."

Along with the reporter, there were now several other people in the foyer, and more yet streaming in through the doors, greeted by a doorman dressed like a Victorian valet. Lacey spotted Councilor Muir standing beside a stone bust of Charles Dickens, nestled in amongst the potted ferns. She was dressed quite extravagantly in a long silky black floor-length dress with matching over-the-elbow gloves, her hair twirled into a neatly coiffed updo. Beside her was a tall, slim man with a moustache, wearing a posh country Englishman's outfit complete with gingham flat cap. Side by side in the conservatory, they looked like a real Victorian couple.

"Oh no!" Suzy said, grasping Lacey's arm.

"What is it?" Lacey asked, following Suzy's gaze over to the couple.

"That's my Uncle Adrian," Suzy said. "Joanie's ex-husband. I totally forgot he said he'd come to support me tonight. My parents are skiing in Switzerland, you see, and my brother is far too competitive to support anything I ever do." She leaned in and spoke in a hushed voice. "We need to separate them."

"Why?" Lacey said, almost laughing. "They're adults. I'm sure they'll be able to put their differences aside for one evening."

"I doubt it," Suzy said, shaking her head. "There's a lot of unresolved financial stuff they're still squabbling about."

Lacey immediately thought of her own ex-husband, and the monthly alimony payments she had to make to him. Their marriage would probably have ended far more amicably had he not gone down that route.

"Please, Lacey," Suzy said. "I don't want them arguing here and ruining my opening night."

It all felt rather childish to Lacey, but she wanted Suzy to have a good night, and if keeping her arguing family members apart was the way to do it, then Lacey would oblige.

"Fine," she said.

"Thank you!" Suzy mouthed.

As they approached, it became immediately obvious the two were in the middle of a heated exchange.

"Three hundred thousand pounds, Ade!" Councilor Muir was hissing. "Of *my* money!"

"*Our* money," the man replied gruffly. "I started that business. A fact you seem to conveniently forget."

"You inherited it," Councilor Muir replied scathingly. "I was the one who ran the damn thing!"

Reaching the pair, Suzy literally stepped between them, facing her uncle. "Uncle Ade, you came!" she exclaimed, throwing her arms around his neck.

At the same time, Lacey wrapped her hand around Councilor Muir's gloved arm, the silk soft on her fingers, and gave her a gentle but firm tug in the other direction.

"I was wondering if I'd run into you here," she said to the woman.

Councilor Muir looked over her shoulder at Uncle Adrian as Suzy maintained her blocking stance. The woman allowed Lacey to guide her away without putting up much protest. She'd probably noticed the reporter and knew that anything even remotely scandalous would make its way into the *Wilfordshire Weekly.*

With expert precision, Suzy and Lacey guided the ex-partners away from one another, and avoided a catastrophe.

"It's nice of you to come and support Suzy," Lacey continued.

Councilor Muir patted down her hair as if to regain her composure. "I support all my constituents' business ventures," she said.

That's rich, Lacey thought. There'd been no sign of the woman when she'd opened the antiques store!

"Oh look, Bill's here," Councilor Muir said, attempting to untangle herself from Lacey's grasp.

Lacey looked over to see a man coming through the glass entryway, nodding hospitably to the doormen. He was wearing a red robe that went past his knees, that had thick gold trim sewn into its velvet collar. Around his neck hung a long golden chain-link necklace.

From around Lacey, she heard a cacophony of excited whispers. "Mayor Fletcher's here?"

It all fell into place. Mayor Fletcher was evidently wearing some kind of traditional attire. To Lacey's non-native eyes, it just made him look a bit like Santa Claus, although his jolly manner and round belly also added to the effect.

So Gina's fake rumor had come true!

Just then, Mayor Fletcher's eyes fell to Councilor Muir and he strolled over with a large smile on his face.

"Bill," Councilor Muir said, taking him by the upper arms and air kissing either side of his gray bushy-bearded cheeks.

"Joan, so nice to see you," he said. He moved away and looked to Lacey. He extended a hand to her. "Hello there. I'm Bill Fletcher."

Lacey felt a bit like she was in the presence of a celebrity. She took his hand in hers and shook it. "You're the mayor."

"What gave it away?" He chuckled. "And you are?"

"Lacey runs the antiques store in town," Councilor Muir jumped in, before Lacey had the chance to answer.

"I know the one!" the mayor replied, pleasantly. "My wife enjoys perusing your store because she is very fond of your dog."

"Chester," Lacey said, smiling broadly, touched she was known by the most important man in Wilfordshire. "He's an English Shepherd."

"We have three dogs at home," the mayor told her. "Every time one of the children left for university, my wife bought another."

Lacey couldn't help but laugh. The mayor seemed very pleasant, and with the same witty sense of humor she was growing accustomed to amongst the townsfolk.

"He's here tonight, actually," Lacey said. "Out in the garden."

"Delightful. I'll have to get a selfie. My wife will be ever so jealous."

Lacey found herself smiling widely. Mayor Fletcher was extremely affable, far from the greedy developer Carol had made him out to be. Perhaps Carol had misunderstood the situation with the redevelopment?

No sooner had Lacey thought her name, than the B&B owner herself appeared, materializing from behind the cloud of spray cast by the fountain.

Lacey immediately gulped. There was only one reason for Carol to have come. She must've heard Gina's rumor about Mayor Fletcher and was here to give him a piece of her mind. A spat between sharp-tongued Carol and Mayor Fletcher would ruin Suzy's evening even more than an argument between her aunt and uncle. Lacey was determined to stop it.

"Excuse me one moment," she said, slipping away from Councilor Muir and the mayor.

She marched toward Carol, who was looking decidedly shifty.

"Carol," Lacey said sharply, coming up in front of her.

Carol flinched as if she'd been caught doing something naughty. Then her eyes flashed with recognition, and her expression hardened. "Lacey. Love what you've done with the place," she said with ice-cold sarcasm.

"You need to leave," Lacey said.

"And miss the fireworks?" Carol replied. "Absolutely not. It's all anyone in town's been talking about all day. In fact, everyone seems more excited about the fireworks tonight than they do about the actual air show tomorrow, which is ironic, because I think I recall you bleating on about how making the air show into a weekend event would benefit the whole town?" She pursed her lips with annoyance. "Looks to me like this whole thing has benefited no one but Suzy. Oh, and you."

Lacey clenched her teeth. Carol had a mean streak to rival Taryn. Lacey could hardly believe she'd once thought of the woman as a friend.

"You and I both know you have no interest in the fireworks," Lacey said. "You're here to accost Mayor Fletcher and—"

Carol cut off her sentence. "Mayor Fletcher is here?" Her eyes were suddenly bulging. "Where? Where is that awful little man?"

She hadn't known? And Lacey had put her big foot in it?

Just then, one of the waiters passed, carrying a silver tray of drinks.

Carol took one and took a huge gulp. "Bit of Dutch courage." Then she started craning her head again.

Lacey thought of Mayor Fletcher's extremely conspicuous red robe. He was like a matador's cloth, and Carol was the furious bull gearing up to charge him.

Carol's eyes suddenly narrowed. She downed the rest of her drink. "There he is," she said suddenly, slamming her glass back onto the silver tray.

The waiter hadn't been anticipating it. He dropped the whole tray, liquid sloshing into the air all over the back of a woman in a black chiffon gown. All the antique glasses smashed across the hard tiled floor.

Lacey crouched down to help the waiter collect the shards of glass. The woman in the black dress who'd been splashed also crouched down to help.

Despite the shock, her toffee-colored hair was still in a perfect Audrey Hepburn do. A thin row of pearls accentuated her delicate collar bone. For a clearly well-to-do lady, she seemed to be taking it remarkably well that she'd just had a whole tray of drinks thrown over her. That was until Lacey realized who it was. Not a well-to-do lady at all ...

"DCI Lewis?" Lacey exclaimed. "Is that you?"

"Oh. Lacey. Hello," the woman replied, stiffly. Despite her glow-up, she still had the exact same mannerisms as usual, with a slightly flattened affect, as if she'd seen far too much in her time.

The women and the waiter hurriedly put all the shards of glass onto the tray.

"What are you doing here?" Lacey asked. Then, with a sudden horrified thought, she quickly added, "Is Superintendent Turner coming?"

DCI Lewis let out a small laugh. It may well have been the first time Lacey had seen her do so.

"I can assure you, Lacey, we're work partners, not socializing partners."

With the glass now cleared, the two women stood.

Lacey realized Carol had disappeared.

"Oh no," she said. "Where's she gone?"

"Who?" DCI Lewis asked.

"Carol. From the B&B. She's going to cause a scene with the mayor."

She glanced around, searching for her. The foyer was extremely busy now. It felt like she was in the audience of a rock concert rather than the opening night of a B&B. Grumpy Greg's advertising scheme had clearly paid off. It seemed like half of Wilfordshire was here.

Lacey's eyes immediately picked out a sight that made her stomach drop to her feet. Tom and Lucia by the grandfather clock giggling away like two teenagers at some shared joke. Lacey ground her teeth. She'd wanted to enjoy this evening with Tom, but instead she was on Mayor-watch while he was busy bonding with the pretty young assistant he was spending the whole day with tomorrow.

"Is that her?" came DCI Lewis's voice.

Lacey followed her point. Sure enough, Carol was there beside a spider plant on her phone. She was waving her arm in a wide arc above her head, trying to get the attention of someone from the entrance.

Lacey looked over to see Ivan Parry entering. He was wearing usual blue jeans and white polo shirt, and was returning his mobile phone to the leather holster at his hip. He was far from dressed for the occasion; Carol must've summoned him here as backup. Ivan had more reason to give the mayor a piece of his mind than anyone.

How many of these crises was Lacey going to have to avoid? Would she ever get a chance to spend any time with Tom at all, or was she going to have to spend the whole evening rushing around keeping enemies away from each other?

"Do you mind distracting Carol?" she asked DCI Lewis. "I've just seen another hazard that needs diffusing."

"Sure. If I can reach her," the detective replied.

They parted ways, DCI Lewis weaving her way through the crowds toward Carol, and Lacey heading the opposite direction in an attempt to cut off Ivan. It was so busy now, she had to use a bit of elbow force to get through. As she went, she reminded herself not to mention the mayor by name, just in case Ivan was here for some other reason.

"Ivan," she said, smiling when she finally reached him. "I wasn't expecting to see you here."

Ivan seemed in his usual good spirits. "Lacey! I'm here to see a friend of mine. Councilor Muir."

"Oh?" Lacey said. Maybe she actually had misunderstood what was going on. Maybe Ivan hadn't been summoned by Carol after all. "You're friends with Councilor Muir?"

"I helped her on her campaign trail at the beginning of the year," Ivan replied with a grin.

"Campaign trail?" Lacey asked.

"For mayor. Oh, I forgot, you didn't move here until spring, did you? Well, Joan went up against Bill Fletcher but lost." His bumbling shyness overcame him. "I mean obviously she lost, because Fletcher's mayor."

Lacey was surprised to learn that Fletcher and Muir had been rivals once. They'd greeted each other like old friends. And from what she'd heard, they both supported the east Wilfordshire regeneration project. Maybe it was a friendly rivalry?

"I'm surprised you'd help her, considering her position on the regeneration of east Wilfordshire."

Ivan's polite exterior faltered at the mention of the hated project. "Joanie's plans were nowhere near as extreme as Bill's. She was going to approve my static holiday home business, for starters. I'm not opposed to progress, Lacey, as long as it's organic. Mayor Fletcher's approach is to take to it with a bulldozer, fill it with chain stores, and ship in outsiders to run the place. I mean, Joanie only approved the business license for the Lodge because it was her niece taking it on, and she has a connection to the area."

Lacey was interested in Ivan's different perspective on the whole thing. Perhaps she'd been a bit too quick to assume it was nepotism that caused the rush on the license. It was probably Carol's snake tongue that had made her even consider it in the first place.

"Have you seen Joan anywhere?" Ivan asked, craning his head over the crowd searching for her.

"I think she was in the garden," Lacey said. "Last I saw she was in the marquee."

But she noticed Ivan's expression had fallen.

"Wait. Is that…?"

Lacey looked over to see Mayor Fletcher chatting away with Uncle Adrian, guffawing at some shared joke.

"He's here!" Ivan exclaimed, his hands clenching into fists. "That bloody dreadful man is here!"

Lacey had never heard anything even remotely hostile come out of Ivan's mouth.

"Please, don't start anything…" Lacey said, apprehension swirled in her guts.

"It's too late for that!" Ivan said. "If the mayor didn't want anything started, he should never have issued me a compulsory purchase order!"

"I know," Lacey said with compassion. She looked at the mayor. He had a big grin on his face. He hid his shady side well. "It's awful. But tonight isn't about the mayor. It's about Suzy."

Ivan didn't seem to be able to hear Lacey at all. He motioned as if to head for the mayor. But at the same time, Grumpy Greg appeared at the foyer door and announced, "Everyone, out to the garden. The fireworks are about to commence!"

The crowds moved immediately, blocking Ivan's path. In a matter of seconds, the mayor had disappeared from sight, swept away with the other hundred or so guests, blending in with the crowd in spite of his large red cloak.

Saved by the fireworks, Lacey thought.

She turned to Ivan. With his moment of fury now broken, he looked a bit embarrassed.

"I should leave," he said.

Lacey nodded kindly. "I think that's for the best."

❧ ❧ ❧

Lacey was relieved to have averted one crisis, but with Carol still on the prowl, her mission was far from complete.

She headed out through the dining room and into the garden. The temperature had dropped a few degrees, even with the heat coming from the barbeque and the enormous number of guests. If she wasn't so tired and worried about Carol, she probably would've been thrilled to know that the upfront costs she'd accrued furnishing the place would be quickly repaid.

She squinted, trying to see if she could catch sight of Carol, but the sky had darkened considerably and the only light came from the inside of the house. Every face was a blurry smudge.

"There she is!" came a voice from beside her.

Lacey felt herself swept up in Tom's warm arms. He spun her around and placed her back on her feet.

Unsurprisingly, Lacey found she'd been deposited right beside Lucia, Tom's shadow for the evening.

"Where have you been?" Tom continued. "I haven't seen you all night!"

"I've been a bit busy trying to stop the small business owners of Wilfordshire from giving the mayor a piece of their mind."

"The mayor is here?" came Gina's voice.

Lacey turned to see Gina with Chester and Boudica either side of her. She was quite relieved they were there; it made her feel less like a third wheel in her own relationship.

"Your rumor came true," Lacey confirmed. "And now Carol's out for blood."

But the others didn't seem to be listening.

"Maybe I'm one of those what-d'you-call-its," Gina was rabbiting. "Clairvoyants?"

Lucia laughed. "Don't clairvoyants talk to the dead?"

"Okay, not one of those then...What do I mean then? Like Nostradamus."

"A seer?" Tom asked.

Just then, the fizz sound of a firework's wick alighting interrupted their idle chatter, and with a whoosh, a rocket took to the sky.

It exploded loudly, lighting the evening sky with sparkles of red.

The dogs began to bark immediately.

"Oh no!" Lacey exclaimed, thinking of Suzy's fear of dogs. After all her attempts to stop other people from ruining Suzy's night, she was going to be the one to ruin it herself!

"Calm down, pups," Gina commanded.

But only Boudica was listening. Chester was freaking out too much. Suddenly, he bolted for the house.

"Chester!" Lacey exclaimed.

She took off after him, shoving her way past the packed bodies of people all staring up to the skies, as the fireworks began exploding in quick succession after her.

My poor petrified pooch! Lacey thought as she ran, admonishing herself for being a bad owner. Of course Chester would hate the fireworks, all animals did. She should've taken him home after work and just been late to the party. She felt terrible for the oversight.

"Chester?" she called, hurrying into the dining room through the folded open glass doors.

There were still a few people inside the room. Obviously not everyone had decided to watch the fireworks display from the garden—the lure of the buffet was too strong.

Lacey just caught sight of Chester up ahead, catapulting through the open door into the corridor. She hurried after him, her heels clicking on the fresh floorboards.

She skidded out into the corridor, but suddenly tripped and fell to her knees. At the exact same moment, the lights cut out.

Wincing in pain from where her knees had collided with the hard wooden floorboards, Lacey realized she must have tripped on one of the extension cords, the ones Greg had been complaining about having to use. She groped forward, trying to find the cable so she could reconnect them.

Before she did, a succession of fireworks began to explode in the garden, one after the next after the next. Their white light was bright enough to illuminate the corridor, and Lacey saw Chester in strobe-like flashes as he leapt up from a cowered position and darted away.

Lacey made the snap decision that her terrified pooch was far more important than fixing the lights, so she got to her feet and hurried after him. She would feel the wrath of Grumpy Greg later, no doubt, but she didn't care. After today, she'd never have to see the miserable man again.

Just then, the stream of fireworks ended, and everything went dark again.

"Chester!" Lacey called, losing sight of him.

She staggered on, quickly disoriented in the unfamiliar building and abject blackness.

Then the fireworks started up again. Red this time, flashing their lights all around like something from a horror movie.

Lacey caught sight of Chester's tail disappearing through an open door and beelined for it while she still had some light to see by.

After several quick *pop pop pops* in a row, there came an enormous *boom,* so loud that Lacey let out a panicked shriek and instinctively ducked down, covering her ears.

Oh, poor Chester! she thought. *If I'm that scared of a firework, imagine how terrified he must be!*

Once again, everything went black and this time an eerie silence accompanied it.

Lacey guided herself along the wall with one hand, aiming for the open door through which she'd seen Chester disappear. But she misjudged the distance and went staggering in through the door, tumbling a little.

All at once, the lamps flickered back on.

Before Lacey had even had a chance to fully work out what room she'd ended up in, a piercing scream sliced through the silence. It took barely a second for her to realize why.

She was in the drawing room. Lying face down, in front of the fireplace, was the mayor. A red pool was radiating from him.

Lacey gasped, her gaze darting up to the other people in the room, who were all staring, gawping at the mayor. Carol, Councilor Muir, Uncle Adrian, Ivan, and Suzy.

Cradled in Suzy's arms was the flintlock rifle.

CHAPTER EIGHT

L acey stared at the mayor's back, where he'd fallen face down. Around him, five people stood.

Suzy dropped the gun. It hit the floor with a loud thud. The noise seemed to snap everyone back to life, and a flurry of activity erupted all at the same time.

"I can't hear anything," Carol was stammering, touching her ears and inspecting her fingers as if expecting blood.

At the same time, Councilor Muir was screeching, "Ambulance! Someone call an ambulance!"

Ivan grabbed his cell phone from its leather hip holster, but he was shaking so hard he dropped it. It went skittering across the floor, hitting Uncle Adrian's feet. He just stared at it, as if he was hypnotized and hadn't really seen it at all.

Lacey hurried forward and pressed her fingers against Mayor Fletcher's neck, searching for a pulse.

"Is he dead?" Suzy squeaked.

Lacey kept searching, using the scant bit of knowledge she had about first aid. She thought she felt a small flutter. Perhaps not all hope was lost.

"I think he's still alive," Lacey said. She looked behind her. "What the hell happened?"

"Someone fired the gun by accident," Uncle Adrian stammered, his eyes darting between the rifle to the still figure lying sprawled on the rug.

"Suzy?" Lacey asked. "Is that what happened? Did you accidentally fire the gun?"

Suzy seemed unable to speak. She opened and closed her mouth like a fish drowning in air, shaking her head over and over. Lacey could see she was shaking like a leaf.

"Is there a doctor here?" Councilor Muir bellowed.

Her voice was far more commanding than Lacey's, and in an instant, the sound of footsteps came thundering toward them.

It felt like a lifetime was passing. Indeed, for the mayor, a lifetime was, because the flicker of a pulse Lacey had felt before was now gone entirely.

She sat back on her heels, realizing it was already too late.

"We need to do first aid," Councilor Muir said. "Move, let me."

She hurried forward, shoving Lacey out of the way with her shoulder.

Lacey shook her head. "It's too late. It's too late. He's gone."

But Councilor Muir wasn't listening.

"Come on, Bill," she said, trying and failing to roll his large body onto its back. "This isn't how it ends. Come on."

Lacey knew it was hopeless, but she let Councilor Muir try, for her own sake.

She looked up behind her, from Uncle Adrian, to Carol, to Ivan, and finally to Suzy. They all looked stunned, Suzy especially. Her baby-deer eyes looked even more frightened than usual.

Suddenly, from the door, a voice bellowed, "Out of the way!" and Doctor Newbury rushed in.

Lacey sprang up to get out of his way, staggering a little as she bumped into Carol.

Then chaos erupted.

The door to the drawing room was suddenly filled with people; all those footsteps Lacey had heard coming had reached them, and now they were swarming like bees from the hive, trying all at once to get inside and see what the cause of all the commotion was. Screams erupted like fireworks all around.

Then Beth Lewis was there, pushing her way through the chaos in her slinky blank evening gown.

"Police!" she yelled. "Let me through."

She crouched down beside Doctor Newbury, the two conferring silently. Lacey saw the swift, barely perceptible shake of the doctor's head, and DCI Lewis's corresponding nod of understanding. Then she craned her head behind her and bellowed, "Everyone out!"

Her words had no effect.

The people who'd crowded inside seemed frozen with shock. Lacey herself was stuck to the spot. It was only the sound of Chester barking that awakened her from her trance.

"Is he dead?" Suzy squeaked again.

DCI Lewis was on her feet now, pushing out with both of her hands. "Get back! Get back!"

"Tell us," Uncle Adrian demanded. "Is Mayor Fletcher dead?"

But Beth was keeping quiet. She was too good an officer to play her cards.

"You're contaminating a crime scene," was all she'd say.

Finally, her words seemed to hit home. All the people who'd rushed in started scrambling now to get back out, though the five people who'd been inside when the gun went off were the farthest from the door, and so Lacey scanned their faces one by one, knowing she was a witness and her evidence would be important.

Carol was pacing, her hands raking through her hair, muttering to herself, "No, no, no." She looked like she couldn't wait to be out of the room. To escape her crime?

Ivan, on the other hand, was completely still. He stood with his eyes averted, his gaze literally on his feet. Too ashamed to bear witness to what he'd done? Hadn't he said he was leaving? Then why was he still here?

Uncle Adrian smoothed his hand over his beard. He looked unfazed by the gun going off in such close proximity, and by the dead body lying by his feet.

Then her eyes flicked again to Suzy, and they locked gazes.

"I didn't do it," Suzy blurted.

Beth Lewis snapped her face toward her, frowning in her hawk-like manner.

"I need you out," the detective said. "Now."

Lacey took Suzy by the hand and tugged her out of the drawing room. As she left, she repeated what Beth Lewis had said in her mind. "You're contaminating a crime scene."

Crime ...? Lacey thought.

Crime seemed to suggest intent. But Mayor Fletcher had been shot accidentally.

She glanced across at Suzy, the woman who'd been holding the smoking gun, and wondered just how much of an accident it really had been.

CHAPTER NINE

L acey staggered into the foyer, her mind spinning.

This can't be happening, she thought, grasping the edge of the stone fountain to steady herself.

Her heart was racing. She turned and sank back, perching her behind on the stone fountain. It was about the worst thing she could have done.

Immediately, the feeling of a fine mist of water on her neck and the chill from the stone seeping through her clothing gave her a terrible sense of déjà vu. It was just like when she'd perched on the rock on the island, with Buck's body lying a few meters away.

She leaped straight back up, her heart pounding in her chest.

What was this recurring nightmare she kept getting stuck in?

"Lacey," came Tom's concerned voice.

She swirled to see him hurrying toward her. The rest of the party-goers (the ones who'd been innocently watching the fireworks display when the gun had gone off) as well as the staff, caterers, and Grumpy Greg, were filing in behind him, speaking in hurried, hushed tones to one another, their expressions vexed. Out in the corridor, Lacey saw DCI Lewis gesturing them into the foyer like a traffic warden, instructing them to please wait until further instructions.

Tom touched Lacey's arm lightly. "What's going on? Beth said there'd been an incident, but won't say anything beyond that."

"It's Mayor Fletcher," she told him. She squeezed her eyes shut. "He's dead."

"What?" Tom exclaimed. "What happened?"

Lacey's mouth felt tacky. "He was shot."

Tom looked aghast. "Shot? How?"

"Suzy must have been showing him the rifle ..." Lacey's voice trailed away as a sudden dawning realization came to her. Suzy hadn't paid for the gun yet. Technically, it was on loan. Lacey was still the registered owner. A hand came up to her mouth. "This is all my fault."

Tom took her by the shoulders. "Don't be silly."

But Lacey was playing it all over again in her mind's eye; Suzy cradling the rifle, the look of deer-like panic on her face. There was no way she'd intended to kill the mayor. She was probably showing off her prized possession, telling everyone in the drawing room its origin story, how it had been the inspiration behind her Victorian hunting lodge theme. Then in the darkness, with the fireworks flashing and Chester running in barking his head off, she must've been spooked.

Lacey felt even more to blame than ever. She was the reason they were in darkness because she'd tripped on the cable. And if Suzy's fear of Chester had caused her to accidentally discharge the rifle, then she was trebly responsible! She was supposed to be in charge of him. She'd promised to keep him on a leash.

She looked up at Tom, feeling an overwhelming fear wash over her. "I'm still the legal owner of the weapon," she stammered. "That means it's my responsibility."

Tom rubbed her shoulders. "It's not your fault, Lacey. You weren't even in the room when it happened."

"But the gun was loaded, Tom!" she exclaimed, as yet more horrible realizations crashed at her. "I didn't even check! I just assumed it wasn't!" She started shaking her head. "Gina was right. I should've been more careful. People can't just go around mounting loaded guns on the wall. They need to be stored properly." All the finickity British laws she'd studied up on when getting her trading license flashed in her mind, and all the different regulations depending on how usable the weapon was. She'd violated several of them.

Panic was rising through her now, and she was starting to draw the attention of the other partygoers. People were looking at her, craning their heads into positions better to hear more salacious details.

"Calm down," Tom told her, his tone somehow both gentle and firm at the same time. "We'll figure this out. I can call my mom for legal advice."

But Lacey was too far gone for reassurances. "I was the one who tripped on the cable!" she said, adding yet more sins to her list, as if she were in Confession. "If I hadn't made it dark, none of this would've happened. If I hadn't brought Chester to a fireworks display, he would never have run off and scared Suzy!"

"Lacey, you're not going down for tripping on a cable. Or for dropping your dog's leash."

"No? You know how Superintendent Turner feels about me. He's never gotten over what happened with Iris Archer, and me showing him up by solving her murder. Any chance he can get to even the score, he will. He'll charge me for improper storage of a firearm. It's written in law. *Reasonable precautions must be taken for the safe custody of the gun(s) and section 1 ammunition*," she recited verbatim. "And if not that, he'll get me for failure to control an animal. What if he has Chester put down?"

Before Tom even got a chance to try to talk her down, at that very moment, Superintendent Turner himself marched into the foyer.

Speak of the devil ...

His effect on the room was immediate. The babble of voices died immediately, as if someone had pressed the mute button. Everyone turned to him expectantly. But Superintendent Turner just stood very still, hands on hips, scowl on face.

His eyes scanned the crowd of witnesses one by one. When he reached Lacey, he stopped, and she saw the moment he registered her with a slightly sinister look of glee flashing in his eyes. *Got you now,* it said.

Lacey's heart started pounding even harder. Her mouth became as dry as a desert.

"What's going on?" someone demanded of the superintendent.

"That's what I'm here to find out," he replied in his typically emotionless tone.

Just then, the sound of wailing police sirens outside grew louder and louder, until the flashing lights of three separate vehicles pulling into the parking lot reflected all around the foyer. The partygoers' silence turned back into a constant hum of confused ruminations.

It felt like it took mere seconds for the elegant foyer to be overrun by police officers. They looked so wrong there, like they didn't belong.

DCI Beth Lewis came in from the corridor where she'd been herding everyone away from the scene, and moved through the crowd toward the colleagues and chief. Her expression was all business, which didn't match with her Cinderella ball gown.

When she reached Superintendent Turner, Lacey just made out her saying, "Everyone's in here now, the house is clear," before the two detectives bent their heads and began conferring between them, blocking her ability to hear.

The police officers divided up, and one broke away through the crowd, heading toward the corridor. He was holding that dreaded blue and white crime scene tape in his hand. The effect of the tape on the partygoers was as immediate as the Superintendent arriving.

"Oh my, is someone dead?" a woman cried.

"Is it murder?" another panicking partier exclaimed.

"I want to leave! Now!" a man demanded.

Superintendent Turner held his hands up to try and silence everyone, though it seemed as if the authority his mere presence had automatically had over the situation was faltering. "Please, everyone, we'll have you on your way home as soon as possible. My officers just need to get statements from everyone, so if you could give them your full cooperation, we'll get this done as quickly as possible. You'll all be allowed home once we've built up an accurate picture."

"An accurate picture of *what*?" bellowed the same furious man who'd demanded he be allowed to leave. "No one's told us what's happened!"

Superintendent Turner looked across at Beth, palming off the more difficult announcement for her to deal with.

"There's been an incident," she said, projecting her voice through the foyer. "Involving Mayor Fletcher. I'm afraid he's dead."

The fallout was instantaneous. Lacey must've heard the word "dead" said about a hundred times in the space of a minute, repeating like some horrible nightmare. The urge to run out of the B&B with her fingers jammed in her ears was overwhelming.

The officers took out their notebooks and began making their way through the crowds, taking down everyone's names. Lacey had been through this enough times now to know what came next. Questioning. Though she had every legal right to leave and not speak to the police, if she didn't, it would look very bad for her. She had no real choice. She was going to have to tell them everything; about the rifle, Chester... and Suzy.

Poor Suzy, Lacey thought, her stomach dropping. The young woman must be reeling. If Lacey had been in her position, she knew she'd never be able to come to terms with accidentally killing a man. Then Lacey realized, in a way, she *was* in Suzy's position. She may not have been the one to accidentally pull the trigger, but her mistakes had caused the event in the first place.

The officers started leading people out of the foyer. Lacey presumed they were separating witnesses in an attempt to stop them contaminating one another's statements. At the same time, a large white van pulled into the parking lot, and a swarm of people emerged. They started dressing in white coveralls and slipping on bright blue disposable shoe coverings. Crime scene analysts. As they entered the foyer, their presence caused a collective, visceral reaction from those still in the foyer. Someone started sobbing.

The crowds parted to let the team of CSA through, everyone stepping back like they were contaminated.

As Superintendent Turner passed Lacey, he gave her a nod. "Lacey. I'm looking forward to hearing your insights."

His dry tone made it evident he was being sarcastic.

Lacey felt her stomach knot.

An officer approached. He had dark auburn hair, and a spattering of orange freckles over his entire face. She recognized him immediately as one of the team of officers who'd arrived on the island the day of Buck's murder.

"We're conducting interviews in separate rooms," he explained. "Would you be willing to come chat with me?"

Lacey knew she had no real choice, and the officer's slip-up in referring to this as an "interview" wasn't lost on her. He might've tried to
cover up his mistake by using the colloquial "chat" after, but by that
point the damage was already done. It didn't take a genius to work out
that Superintendent Turner had fingered her as a possible suspect; the
officer had addressed her first rather than Tom, after all, or any of the
other partygoers who'd been in closer proximity, come to think of it.
She'd been singled out.

From his position beside her, Tom reached out and squeezed her hand
reassuringly. She wished it could've made her feel better, but it didn't.

She followed the officer hypnotically. He led her toward the reception
desk that had been placed strategically to stop guests from wandering
behind the scenes into the back offices, storerooms and kitchen, opened
up the hatch, and gestured her through. Lacey assumed they'd be heading
for the office. But instead, the man directed her into the kitchen.

It was a huge place, the one room they'd left untouched during the
renovation since it was perfectly functional for the B&B's needs, if not a
little dated. Everything was battered stainless steel. Gray and ugly. It was
also very messy, since the caterers had obviously been working flat-out
on their canapes at the time of the shooting. On the side stood the large
patisserie box containing Lucia's *marvelous* cake.

Lacey knew there was only one reason why the kitchen had been
chosen as the site of her "chat" when there were at least six bedrooms,
and several offices that would have made far more comfortable surround-
ings for a potentially traumatized witness. They *wanted* her to be uncomfortable. Just like the interrogation room in the police station...

They sat on stools at the shiny metal counter. Silence fell.

Lacey drummed her fingers against the counter, impatient, awkward.
"Aren't you going to ask me any questions?"

"Why don't *you* begin?" the officer said.

It was just like counseling, Lacey thought. They sit back and let you
lead the way. It had always made her feel uncomfortable as a teenager
when her bereavement counselor did it, (though she'd never really been
onboard with the process anyway, since her father was missing, not
dead), and it made her feel uncomfortable now. Only here, making her

uncomfortable was probably their goal. Well, they were doing a damn fine job of it.

Gina's voice floated into Lacey's mind then, saying, "A *bloody* fine job," and Lacey found herself smiling in spite of everything.

"Is something amusing?"

Lacey's gaze snapped to the other side of the room. Superintendent Turner was standing there, having silently come in through the swinging adjoining door between the dining room and kitchen.

Of course, Lacey thought, every single muscle in her body tensing, *the boss wants to question me himself...*

She pursed her lips as he took a stool opposite her. She would never get through this now, Superintendent Turner keeping a hawk-like focus on her every move, word, and even her mannerisms.

"I already gave my statement to Beth," she said curtly, before he had a chance to begin.

"Do you mean DCI Lewis?" he replied, without missing a beat. He produced a note pad and flipped through the pages. "Yes, I've read your statement. Interesting reading. A lot of coincidences." He looked up at her, his eyes beady. "Seems like you may well be the most important witness in this whole B&B. Again. You either have very bad luck, or you're a magnet for it."

Lacey stayed silent. She knew he was trying to rile her, by insinuating that she purposefully injected herself into all the terrible things that had happened recently.

Superintendent Turner's stool squeaked beneath him as he adjusted his large frame. He peered back down at the notebook.

"Fido," he said, using his nickname for Chester. "I see he was the one who found the body."

Lacey folded her arms, unimpressed. "I don't think you're reading it correctly. Chester was present when the lights came back on and the body was revealed, but he wasn't the only one to see it. There were others in the room."

"We'll get back to them," Superintendent Turner said. "I'm interested in these lights. Tell me about them."

"They'd been turned off."

"Turned off? As in someone flicked the switch? In a room with thick velvet curtains that were drawn? In a room lit by several lamps?"

Lacey started to feel a tightening in her throat. It was as if Superintendent Turner had read the guilt in her eyes about tripping over the cable.

"Maybe. Or maybe the electricity went," Lacey said.

"Huh," the Superintendent said. "I'm right in thinking you had a large role in getting the B&B up and running. Is that correct?"

"Yes."

"So you know about the internal layout of the building? Which rooms are where. Their square footage. Where the power outlets are…"

The tightening in her throat started to feel like a noose. He must know. But how?

Then she realized. The lights came back on after the gun had fired. Someone must've found the two halves of the cable and reattached them. But there was no way Turner could know that she was the one who accidentally pulled them apart in the first place. There could only be one answer: someone had seen her in the corridor, chasing after Chester, and they'd given her name to the police as the person who'd killed the lights.

Lacey was caught in an impossible conundrum.

"I don't have it committed to memory," she said, evasively. "But I can show you my detail sketches if you want accurate measurements."

He smirked at her obvious attempt to elude the real question. "So you don't know where the power outlets were?"

He'd caught her now. If Lacey said she didn't, it would come back to bite her later. She had to be honest, no matter how incriminating it made her look.

"There was some discussion about there not being enough. The strip lights were taken out but there wasn't time to replace them, so we used lamps. That took up a significant portion of the outlets, which meant the events planner had to use extension cords. Perhaps the system was accidentally overloaded and that's why the lights tripped out?"

Superintendent Turner started to chuckle. "I wondered how long it would take before you offered up one of your theories." He leaned back, putting his hands behind his head. "Go on, please, I'd like to hear more."

The ginger-haired police officer looked awkward, like he wanted to be anywhere but here witnessing this extremely frosty exchange. As far as he understood it, Lacey was a potential suspect. Superintendent Turner was treating this interview like she was a proven murderer.

"I don't have any theories," Lacey said, calmly, trying her best not to rise to the bait. "All I know is what I saw. The mayor lying face down, dead beside the fireplace. And the people who were standing around him."

"Yes, the other people. Let's go through them, shall we? There was you and Fido the dog. Then we have Carol from the B&B and Ivan Parry. Two people in the tourist industry who hated the mayor."

"Hate is a strong word," Lacey interjected.

"Two people in the tourist industry who weren't very fond of the mayor. Who were particularly hostile toward his plans for redevelopment, weren't they? Ivan was set to lose a lot of money because of the rezoning change. And Carol's been opposed to the redevelopment plan for years."

"So I've been told."

He flicked through Lacey's written statement again. "Councilor Muir was present."

"Yes, that's right."

"And ... Uncle Adrian? Is that *your* uncle Adrian?"

"I don't have an Uncle Adrian, and if I did, he would be in America, wouldn't he? That's Suzy's Uncle Adrian. That's how I was introduced to him this evening, so when I gave my statement that was just the name that came out."

"Suzy," Superintendent Turner said, changing tack as he was wont to do when he felt outsmarted. "She was the final person. And I believe you said someone was holding a gun." He made a point of leafing through the pages of the statement, even though it was obviously right there in front of him. He just needed it from the horse's mouth, so to speak. "Who was that again ... ?"

Lacey wanted the ground to swallow her up. The last thing she wanted to do right now was repeat, again, that she'd seen Suzy holding the gun. Once to Beth Lewis felt like helpful information, but to Superintendent

Turner and his ginger-haired crony, it felt like throwing Suzy under the bus. But there was no getting around it. Suzy had been the one holding the gun and it was already committed to paper.

Except…

"She was cradling it!" Lacey exclaimed. "She wasn't holding it in a way someone would if they'd just fired it. It was as if… as if someone had shoved into her arms."

"I'm sorry?" Superintendent Turner asked.

"I don't think Suzy fired the gun. I think someone else shot the mayor, then shoved the gun into her arms."

She felt a surge of relief to know her friend wasn't responsible for the death of a man.

"Maybe we should leave Suzy to explain herself what happened, and stick to what we know to be facts?" Superintendent Turner said, testily. "The gun."

"What do you want to know about the gun?" Lacey asked.

"It's yours, I understand."

"That's correct. It's on loan to the B&B. It's classified as an ornamental antique."

"Last time I checked, ornaments don't kill people."

Lacey wanted to make a quip about Professor Plum in the billiard room with the candlestick, but decided it was unwise.

"Was there a question?" she asked.

From beside Superintendent Turner, the ginger-haired police officer coughed into his fist, clearly a little amused by her boldness. But Lacey felt buoyed by what she'd worked out about Suzy.

Superintendent Turner snapped his notebook shut. He looked annoyed. "No. No question. I think we're done here."

"I can go home?"

The detective didn't make eye contact with her as he nodded and shooed her away. Lacey looked at the police officer instead. He seemed wholly embarrassed by his chief's behavior and quickly said, "Thanks for your cooperation."

Lacey couldn't get out of there quickly enough.

❧   ❧   ❧

Chester trotted beside Lacey as she staggered down the front steps of the Lodge. Air chilled the perspiration that had formed on her neck during Superintendent Turner's grilling session. She'd been inside the B&B for so long, the light had faded entirely, and night had driven out the warmth of the day.

As she retrieved her cell phone from her pocket, she saw it was almost one a.m.

She looked around and noticed that while she was the only person in the parking lot, she'd not been the first allowed to leave; she could tell because there was an empty space when before there had been none. The vintage red Beetle that belonged to Grumpy Greg was missing. His interview with the police must've been rather quick, Lacey thought bitterly, recalling her own stressful encounter.

She wondered how long it would be before Tom, Gina, and Lucia made an appearance and they could get home. Her bed had never seemed so appealing.

As she stared down at the illuminated screen, a message popped onto it. It was from her mother. And she hadn't sent it to the usual family thread, but privately, and to Lacey alone.

What is this about your father and a gun?

The temperature seemed to drop another two degrees. If she'd thought she'd been in a tailspin, she was in an even greater one now.

"Bloody Naomi!" she said aloud, the word *bloody* coming out quite naturally.

The message she'd sent her little sister was supposed to be between the two of them. But of course her drama-prone little sister had immediately passed it on to their mother. The last thing Lacey wanted was her mom knowing she was trying to find out what happened to her father all those years ago, and dredge up all that pain it had taken so many years to process and move on from.

An antiques contact of mine met Dad once and thought he'd said something about rifles. That's all.

She hoped the way she'd framed it would be sufficient enough to quench her mom's appetite, but nothing she said usually did so she wasn't holding out much hope. She waited, cell phone in hand, for some emotionally charged response from her mom, but none came.

She clicked on the message, double-checking it had sent. It had. Two blue ticks told her it had been read on the other end.

As her eyes lingered on the message, the words "antiques contact" seemed to grow bolder.

Xavier. This was his fault. The rifle he'd sent her had been loaded! What kind of hapless decision making had led him to send her a loaded gun?

Her blood boiling, and barely thinking about what she was doing, she scrolled through her contacts until she found Xavier's number. It was already 2 a.m., and Spain was ahead, but Lacey didn't care. His stupid gift had gotten someone killed! She hit the dial button.

Lacey listened to the phone ring through the speaker, tapping her foot impatiently. Filtering through the doors came a couple of bewildered-looking guests. She hoped Tom, Gina, and Lucia would be through fairly soon; she'd better make this call quick.

"Lacey?" came a sleepy voice in her ear. It had been over a month since she'd heard Xavier's voice. She'd forgotten how smooth and soothing his Spanish accent was. "What's the matter?"

"What's the matter is your gun's been used in a crime. Why didn't you tell me it was loaded?"

"Wait. What?"

Through the phone, she could hear the shuffling sound of fabric; Xavier must have sat bolt upright from the shock.

Serves him right, Lacey thought. This is all his fault.

"I said that the gun you sent me was loaded," she repeated. "And now someone's been shot."

"I don't understand!" Xavier exclaimed. "I wouldn't have sent you a loaded gun, Lacey. Absolutely not."

"Then how do you explain the dead man with a bullet hole in his chest?"

Her fury was met by silence. Xavier must have been stunned into silence.

"Lacey, I promise you," he said finally, his tone firm. "That gun was not loaded. I checked it myself. I would never have been so foolish as to courier a loaded weapon! If the man was shot, then someone else must have loaded it."

For the first time, his words started to sink in.

Someone else loaded the gun.

And that could only mean one thing. The gun wasn't fired by accident at all. There was no mishap because of the lights cutting out, or Chester's shrill barks surprising someone.

Suzy hadn't accidentally shot the mayor. The mayor had been murdered.

There was a liar amongst the drawing room five.

On the other end of the phone, Xavier was still speaking; apologizing, it seemed, for all the trouble he'd caused. But Lacey couldn't hear a word he said. She'd turned her focus back to the brightly lit glass foyer at the front of the B&B, and the figure being led out of it in handcuffs; arrested not on manslaughter, but murder.

Suzy.

CHAPTER TEN

It was four in the morning by the time Lacey used her Rapunzel key to get back into Crag Cottage, a bleary-eyed Tom and snoozy Chester by her side.

After the police had allowed everyone to leave, Tom had insisted on driving Lucia back to her apartment—even though the girl said she could just call a cab—and the roundabout journey had taken ages. Lucia bawled in the backseat the whole while, wailing, "I just can't believe they arrested Suzy! She wouldn't say boo to a fly!"

After fulfilling his Knight in Shining Armor duties by depositing Lucia safely inside her apartment, Tom had driven Lacey, Gina, and a loudly snoring Chester to their cliffside cottages. He took the winding narrow road to Gina's house first—again, despite her insistence she could walk the last few feet herself. Tom must've been feeling extra protective, Lacey reasoned, which was understandable considering a man was lying dead.

Needless to say, a sense of delirious, exhausted relief overcame Lacey as she shoved open the door of Crag Cottage and took a step inside the dark, cold entryway. Lacey had been working so hard she had not been home to use the Aga to make dinner, and that was the old cottage's main heating source.

Tom entered behind her and shivered.

"You have to leave for work in two hours," Lacey said between chattering teeth. She kicked off her heels, cursing herself silently for having worn them in the first place.

"I think tomorrow's going to be a pretty crappy day," Tom said, with brazen honesty.

They walked the length of the low-ceilinged corridor and stepped down into the cozy cottage kitchen. Moonlight streaked through the window and across the tiled floors. Lacey slumped into a chair at the kitchen table.

"Glittery rainbows, hymns, and low-flying airplanes," Tom added, as he headed for the fridge.

"I'm sure Luce will help you through it," Lacey mumbled, dropping the heavy weight of her head into her hands.

"If she makes it," came Tom's voice from behind the fridge door, evidently having failed to notice the pointedness in Lacey's comment. He reemerged holding two beer bottles. "She seemed like she was in quite a state. I might have to give her the day off and take … Paul." He shuddered.

Lacey was quietly glad Tom hadn't picked up on the veiled accusation in her comment. She knew she was taking out her frustration on the easiest target. Now really wasn't the time for her petty jealousies. Not when there were more pressing matters to attend to.

"Poor Mayor Fletcher," Lacey said. "He has a wife. Children. Dogs. He seemed like a good man, even if his decisions about Wilfordshire weren't to everyone's tastes."

Tom took the seat opposite Lacey and set the two bottles of beer he'd collected from the fridge down on the table before them. The last thing Lacey wanted was more alcohol, so she shook her head when he offered one to her.

He popped the lid of his own. "Can you think of any reason why Suzy …" He paused, beer bottle hovering beside his lips, as he attempted to find the right words. "… would wish to harm him?"

His tiptoeing around the subject made his comment no less rude to Lacey. She shot him an incredulous look.

"Suzy didn't do this!" she exclaimed.

"But she was the one holding the gun," he said, simply. "I mean, she was *literally* holding the smoking gun."

He took a swig of beer, looking somewhat pleased with himself.

Lacey narrowed her eyes and gave her head an exaggerated shake. "Actually, she wasn't *holding* the smoking gun. She was *cradling* it. It looked to me like someone had shoved it into her arms. That's not how you hold a gun you've just discharged."

Over the lip of his beer bottle, Tom raised an eyebrow skeptically.

"I'm certain, Tom," Lacey said, more firmly. "Suzy had no motive. No reason. She's not a killer."

Tom gently placed his glass bottle back onto the table. He reached over and touched Lacey's hand lightly. "You said the same thing about Brooke."

Immediately, Lacey wrenched her hand out from under his, hurt he'd even make such a comment. "This is a completely different situation! Just because I made the wrong judgment call before doesn't mean I'm making it again. Suzy is not Brooke." She could hear her own voice rising with passion. "Suzy was framed. Someone else in that room killed Mayor Fletcher."

Tom regarded her, his eyes searching hers. Finally, he stood. "All right then. If you're so certain, let's go through this logically."

Lacey watched him cross the kitchen to the counter and fetch a pen and notepad. He returned to his seat, flipped over to a fresh page, and wrote *The Drawing Room Five*.

"Tom," Lacey said reproachfully. "This isn't a movie. It's serious. A man is dead."

Tom held his hands up innocently. "I'm not messing around. I promise. So, tell me. Who was there?"

"Adrian," Lacey began, still a little skeptical that Tom was taking this as somberly as he ought to. Like most English men, his tendency towards gallows humor didn't sit well with her.

"What do we know about him?" Tom asked as he noted down his name.

"He's Suzy's uncle," Lacey told him. "They share a surname, so I'd assume he's her father's brother. He was once married to Joan Muir, but they divorced about ten years ago. And I guess he's supportive enough of his niece to come to her launch party as the family representative."

Tom finished scribbling what she'd said, and Lacey read the upside down notations: *–family oriented?*

"Who else?" Tom asked.

Lacey felt a squirming in her stomach as she announced the next suspect. "Ivan."

Tom hid his surprise well, but it didn't get past the ever perceptive Lacey. The way he carefully added his name to the list lacked the same enthusiastic flourish as he'd had when writing Adrian's. Maybe now that he realized this was going to affect real people they knew, he would take it a bit more seriously, Lacey thought.

"Well, we can pretty much rule him out right away," Tom said. "A landlord who needs to be negotiated *up* on the rent so he can at least break even is hardly going to murder a man!"

The squirming in Lacey's stomach grew worse. "He was furious with Mayor Fletcher, though," she told him, hating to admit it. "The mayor's regeneration plans were going to ruin him."

"Even so, you and I both know Ivan couldn't kill anyone," Tom said, poised to cross his name out. "The worst Ivan would do is write a strongly worded open letter to the *Wilfordshire Gazette*. Even then it would be filled with apologies. But then again, desperate people do desperate things ..."

Though his pen was still poised to strike out Ivan's name, Lacey could see the confidence in his face begin to falter.

"Not everyone is as they seem," he said finally.

Evidently, Lacey thought. Because whatever way it was sliced, *someone* in that room had chosen to murder a man in cold blood.

"Who else was there?" Tom prompted.

"Suzy, of course," Lacey said, tapping her middle finger to indicate the third person.

Tom added her name to the list. He didn't ask for any extra details. Obviously, he was starting to wake up to the reality of the situation.

"Then we have Councilor Muir," she continued. "But I'm pretty sure it wasn't her."

"Why? Fletcher and Muir were rivals during the mayoral elections, weren't they? She lost out to him. That gives her a motive. A stronger one than any of the others, if you ask me."

Lacey wasn't convinced. "They're friends. Any rivalry between them is all in good faith."

"How can you be so sure?"

"I saw them greet one another at the party, First names. Air kisses. There was genuine affection between them."

Tom rolled his eyes. "Genuine affection? Between politicians?" He spoke with a wry, sarcastic tone. "Considering there was a reporter there from the *Weekly Wilfordshire*, I'd take any of their public behavior with a grain of salt."

"Fine," Lacey said. "I hear your point. It could've all been for show. But Councilor Muir was the first one to react when the lights came back on. She called out for an ambulance. She tried to give him CPR, even when he was obviously beyond saving. You can't fake that kind of compassion."

Her words seemed to give Tom pause for thought. He jotted down – *friend* beside Councilor Muir's name.

"It doesn't make sense that she'd shoot a man and then attempt to save his life," Tom said. Then his head snapped up with sudden excitement. "Unless it was all some carefully constructed PR stunt, so she could be the heroine."

"Tom…" Lacey warned. She could see he was about to get ahead of himself with wild theories lacking any logical evidence. "If Muir wanted to play the save-the-day heroine, there are safer ways to go about it than with a rifle in a darkened room."

"You're right," Tom said, looking disappointed that his flight of fancy had been taken apart so quickly by Lacey. "Who was the final person?"

Lacey didn't want to admit the final suspect was Carol. Because Tom knew as well as anyone else in Wilfordshire just what Carol thought of Mayor Fletcher. And he knew all about her meltdown in Lacey's store over the B&B, and her subsequent outburst at Lacey for taking on the decorating work there.

"It was Carol," Lacey finally said, her voice dropping.

"Ah," Tom said, with an air of understanding. He kept his focus on the notepad. "Carol."

"Yeah," Lacey said with a resigned sigh.

With her name there in black and white, it seemed so obvious that Carol was the prime suspect. Not just because of how furious she was with Mayor Fletcher, but because of how much anger she also directed at Suzy. Why not kill two birds with one stone, by murdering the source of her pain and framing her stiffest competition?

"But if it's so obviously Carol…" Tom said, "why was Suzy the one being led away in handcuffs?"

"I don't know," Lacey said, shrugging. "Because they're idiots." She retracted her statement immediately. "Actually, Superintendent Turner's an idiot. Beth's actually pretty sound, she just gets overruled by him all the time. Beth probably told him that Suzy was holding the gun, and he got tunnel vision after that. He'll be busy trying to find evidence to fit the narrative now, just like he did with Xavier."

Tom paused and quirked his head to the side. "With who?"

Lacey pressed her lips together. She was so tired she'd lost focus on who she was talking to. Now she'd walked straight into a tricky situation.

"Xavier," she repeated, hearing the strain in her voice as she attempted to play it off innocently. "The Spanish man. The police were looking into him when Buck died. You remember?"

"Vaguely," Tom said. "Gosh, that feels like a million years ago!"

"It really does," Lacey agreed.

She felt heavy and weary, and more than a little lost. She'd spent the last week working so hard, she'd never in a million years imagined this would be the outcome of it all.

"Oh no, Tom!" she suddenly exclaimed, reaching out and grabbing his hand.

"What? What's wrong?"

"I've just thought, the B&B will be closed. It's an active crime scene, and its owner is in police custody. Suzy was counting on booking guests off the back of the launch party to start generating an income. That's why we worked flat out to get everything done in time for the air show, because that would give people a reason to want to stay the weekend in Wilfordshire. But now, and for however long this investigation takes place, the B&B won't be making a single dime."

"Penny," Tom corrected. "And I really don't think losing out on a bit of income is at the top of Suzy's worries right now."

"Not Suzy's income!" Lacey cried. *"Mine!"* The panic started to creep through her now. "Tom, I fronted thousands and thousands of dollars for the merchandise. It's all on my card. There's no way I'll make that money back. I'll default on the house payment. I might even have to sell the store."

"It will be okay," Tom told her.

But his attempts to reassure her fell on deaf ears. With the sudden realization that her entire livelihood was tied to the B&B and the outcome of the investigation, Lacey's terrible evening had just gotten much, much worse.

CHAPTER ELEVEN

Lacey felt Chester's nose nudging into her side. She groaned and rolled over in bed. Her canine companion had his paws up on the mattress and was looking at her expectantly.

The side of the bed where Tom slept when he stayed over was empty. He'd left for work at five thirty, Lacey recalled, remembering him accidently waking her, and being grouchy with him about it.

She glanced over at the alarm clock. It was eight AM. In a flurry, she threw back the covers and sat bolt up. Gina had forgotten to pick Chester up on her way to work. So much for her plans for a Saturday lie-in.

"Chester!" she exclaimed, heaving her weary body out of bed. You're late for your walkies."

All the drama of the night before must have caused it to slip Gina's mind. Not that Gina needed an excuse to forget things, Lacey thought. She was scatter-brained at the best of times.

As Lacey tugged on her dressing gown, bits and pieces of the evening before returned to her. By the time she was dragging herself downstairs, her woeful predicament over the perilous state of her finances made her stomach twist into knots.

Chester followed Lacey into the kitchen, an expectant expression on his face.

She checked her phone. There'd been a message from Gina apologizing for forgetting to collect Chester and reminding Lacey not to come to work until at least lunch time, advice Lacey was promptly about to ignore.

Lacey messaged back with one hand saying she was on her way, but taking the long route along the beach—since sea air was great to wake up tired bodies, and ocean views were perfect for contemplative states about one's suddenly dire finances—while she brewed a coffee shop's worth of coffee with the other, so it could percolate while she was showering. Then she dragged herself back upstairs, Chester trotting up after her and waiting outside the door the whole time.

Back in her room, Lacey didn't feel like putting on her work attire today. She had bad memories attached to them now. Instead, she opted for a pair of comfy jeans and a thin sweater.

"What do you think, Chester? One dress down day never hurt anyone."

He whinnied.

"I know, I know, I'm sorry, boy. Let's go."

She went into the kitchen, topped up the coffee with cold water, then downed it—Chester watching with his head tipped to the side as if in disbelief that he *still* wasn't on his walkies—then she finally reached for his leash from its hook beside the back door.

Chester went wild, barking and turning in circles. Lacey couldn't help but smile.

"You've been very patient," she told him.

She clipped Chester into his leash and left Crag Cottage via the back door, walking the length of the back garden until they reached the fence and the steps that led down the cliff face directly to the beach.

It seemed much busier than usual today, and Lacey put it down to the fact she was setting out later than normal, and the fact that it was forecast to be a super warm day. But then a sudden noise from behind made Lacey jump.

She turned, shocked, and saw a formation of old war planes soaring through the sky over the island toward her.

"The air show…." she said aloud, having completely forgotten about it.

She peered up at the cliffs and saw rows of spectators. How long would it take before the news broke of the mayor's murder? What would it do to the tourists who'd come to the town for the day?

Another plane soared overhead, fairly low, and very loud. Unlike with the fireworks, Chester seemed completely unfazed by the planes.

He'd obviously gotten used to the annual show of his town, whereas being right by a fireworks display was new, strange, and unfamiliar.

She was halfway along the route when she felt her phone start vibrating. The number was one she was sadly well acquainted with. Wilfordshire police station.

Frowning, Lacey answered the phone. "Yes?"

"Lacey, it's DCI Lewis," came the voice on the other end. "Would you be able to come down to the station?"

"Why?" Lacey asked, suspiciously. They'd played this trick on her before, asking her to come in as a witness then turning her into a suspect. It was only thanks to Tom's mom, Heidi, that her last trip to the police station hadn't turned into a three-day lock-up.

"We're planning on releasing Suzy from custody, but she doesn't have an address in town, and conditions of her release are that she checks in every six hours. So we need someone to agree to provide her a place to stay. She suggested you might be able to help."

Lacey was relieved to hear Suzy was being released. She was also touched. And, if she had to be honest, a little smug that Suzy had chosen her over her childhood friend Lucia.

"If you're releasing her," Lacey said, "does that mean you know it wasn't her?"

The sooner Suzy was free and back in the B&B, the sooner the rumor mill would be silenced and the less damage the whole ordeal would do. She may even be given the all clear to start renting the rooms, and the out-of-town tourist trade she was appealing to would have no reason to avoid booking one if they knew nothing of the man who'd died inside its drawing room. Maybe Lacey's bill would be paid on time after all?

Beth Lewis was silent for a moment. "There's not enough evidence pointing to her." Then hurriedly she added, "In my opinion."

Lacey knew DCI Lewis had to keep professional, although she always felt something of an affinity with the female detective. It often felt like Beth was on the same page as her, and that Lacey could give her the moral support her superior failed to.

Lacey was about to tell Beth not to worry, she wouldn't pry. But before she could, the detective blurted out, "Her fingerprints didn't match the trigger. The only place we found hers was on the barrel."

"Oh," Lacey said, surprised with the amount of information Beth was willing to reveal.

But then it occurred to her what must be happening. Once again, she was butting heads with Superintendent Turner.

"I'm on my way," Lacey told her.

She hung up the call and diverted toward the police station.

When she got there, she was surprised by a familiar face standing in the reception area. It was Tom's mother, Heidi.

"What are you doing here?" Lacey asked, puzzled by her presence.

She wished she hadn't chosen today to wear her unflattering jeans and sweater combo, and have unstyled hair and probably dark purple bags under her eyes from having barely slept for a week. It wasn't like their first meeting had gone particularly well, and they'd had very little chance to spend any time together since.

"I heard about the mayor," Heidi said, cordially. "I came to help your friend."

Before Lacey had a chance to ask how she knew it was her friend who needed help, Heidi turned to face the bulletproof glass that separated the reception staff from the waiting room. Behind it stood Superintendent Turner.

"This ignorant man seems to think he can bend and twist the law to suit his needs," Heidi continued. She cast cold eyes at the superintendent.

"We have enough evidence to keep Suzy inside," he said. "And a witness statement saying she was seen holding the gun." He smirked at Lacey, the witness who'd made the statement.

Lacey gulped.

Just then, she noticed Beth Lewis lurking behind her superior, trying to catch her eye. She immediately understood what the female detective was attempting to silently communicate to her. She'd dropped a very large hint during their telephone conversation after all.

"Have you taken her fingerprints?" Lacey asked Superintendent Turner. "I mean, you fingerprinted me about five minutes after I was arrested, so…"

"Yes, of course we have," Superintendent Turner. "We follow protocol here, despite what you seem to think of us."

"So did it match the weapon?" Lacey asked.

Hovering behind Karl Turner's shoulder, Lacey saw a small smile twitch up the corners of Beth's lips.

"We have a matching print, yes," he replied, testily, folding his arms.

"On the trigger?" Lacey prompted.

Superintendent Turner pressed his lips together. "I can't discuss an ongoing investigation with a random member of the public," he said curtly.

Heidi stepped forward. "But you can discuss it with the defendant's lawyer, can't you?" She smirked and adopted the same power pose as Lacey; expectant, eyebrow raised, arms folded.

Turner sighed. "Fine. No, her prints were not found on the trigger. But they are on the murder weapon."

"Of course they are," Heidi retorted immediately. "It's her possession! I'd be more suspicious if her prints *weren't* on the rifle, since that would suggest a clean-up."

Turner sucked his cheeks in like he'd tasted sour lemon. He ignored Heidi and focused his attention on Lacey. "You placed her at the scene of the crime, holding the murder weapon, immediately after the sound of gunfire, where an injured man was discovered bleeding out on the floor. So why don't you and your stupid doggy sidekick go and play your games elsewhere, and let the professionals do their work?"

Chester growled.

"Don't assume what I'm thinking, Superintendent Turner," Lacey said. "You're not a mind reader."

Heidi stepped forward. "I think it's quite evident that Susannah Rowe needs to be released right now, as per the original document put together by DCI Lewis. We have her nominated guardian here to sign that she'll return her to the station for six hourly check-ins, and I'm her legal representative signing an agreement to the conditions. And what's this?" She plucked a pen from her top pocket. "I even have a biro to sign it with!"

Lacey couldn't help herself from smirking. Heidi's sarcastic sense of humor was so much like Tom's.

"Where's the document, then?" she added. "I'm waiting."

Superintendent Turner pouted. He'd been defeated. He retrieved the document, slammed it on the desk, then marched away, leaving the three women to exchange triumphant glances.

CHAPTER TWELVE

acey's prideful moment was short-lived. The moment Suzy was led out into the reception area, she saw the tormented expression on her friend's face. She was pale. Frightened. All the bubbly enthusiasm Lacey had come to expect from her had vanished entirely.

The enormity of what she was going through seemed to erase her dog-phobia as well, because when she saw Lacey waiting for her in the waiting room, she rushed up to her, even though Chester was right there by her feet. She fell into Lacey's arms and let out a little choked sob, seemingly oblivious to Chester's attempts to console her by rubbing his head against her calves.

"I'm so sorry," Suzy squeaked.

"Sorry for what?" Lacey said, kindly. "You've done nothing wrong."

"For dragging you out here. For crying."

"I'm not scared of tears," Lacey told her gently. "You let it all out."

The kindness was all the invitation Suzy needed. A great torrent of sobbing was unleashed.

Heidi stood beside the two women, wearing a sympathetic expression, her gaze politely averted.

"I ... I can't believe Mayor Fletcher is really dead," Suzy murmured into Lacey's sweater. "I feel so responsible."

Heidi stepped up and touched Suzy's arm. She told her, in a stern but quiet voice, "Best to chat outside." She pointed subtly at the CCTV cameras dotted around the waiting room, capturing their every move.

Suzy moved back out of Lacey's arms and looked confused. But Lacey got it right away. The cameras were always rolling, ready to catch people out. Even saying she *felt* responsible could be enough ammo for

Superintendent Turner to follow a confession route and get her locked up again.

"I don't mean to be rude, but who are you?" Suzy asked, wiping her tears off her nose with the back of her hand.

"This is Heidi," Lacey said, introducing her. "She's Tom's mom. She's an excellent lawyer, so you're in great hands."

"But I didn't hire a lawyer," Suzy said.

"My son called me," Heidi explained. "He said you were a friend in need."

Lacey was even more stunned by the admission than she'd been when she first saw Heidi in the station. Just a few hours earlier, Tom had been sitting at her kitchen table accusing Suzy himself. He must've seen how adamant Lacey was about Suzy being innocent and changed his tune. Or maybe it was her panic over her impending financial doom that had prompted him into action. Either way, Lacey was touched. It showed some startling perceptiveness on Tom's part; perceptiveness that was sadly lacking when it came to all matters related to Lucia...

"Well, thank you for getting me out," Suzy said to Heidi. "But my parents are going to send in the family's lawyer to help me."

Lacey raised her eyebrows. She knew Suzy came from wealth, but wealthy enough for the family to have their own lawyer? That made her, to quote Gina, *bloody* wealthy!

They headed out of the police station and down the steps.

"I'm so tired," Suzy said, yawning.

Lacey rubbed her arm for comfort. "I bet you are. Come on, let's get you into a nice warm bed. We can take a taxi back to my place. I'm sure you're too tired to walk."

"I can give you a lift," Heidi offered. Then, putting on a Texas cowgirl accent, self-corrected herself with, "*I can give you a ride.*"

Lacey wasn't sure if Heidi was mocking her or not. It was hard to know where she stood with Tom's mother. Not that Heidi had ever said anything about Lacey's loopiness last time, but Lacey still had it at the back of her mind that she probably wasn't thrilled her son was in a relationship with her. Hopefully, she'd redeemed herself a little in the woman's eyes during the events of the morning.

They all got in Heidi's car and headed to Crag Cottage. Chester sat in the middle seat between Suzy and Lacey. Suzy didn't protest, not even when he rested his head against her shoulder. The poor thing had been through such an ordeal, she didn't even have the energy to be afraid.

On the drive, Lacey received a message from Gina. *Everything okay? You've been ages. I thought your walk would be done by now.*

Slight change of plans, Lacey texted back. *I'm with Suzy and Heidi. We just picked her up from the station and are taking her back to the cottage.*

Are you crazy???? Gina replied immediately. *She might be a murderer!!!*

Lacey couldn't help the irritation Gina's comment induced in her. She texted back simply, *She's not.*

Then she put her phone in her pocket and ignored the subsequent vibrations that told her Gina was on a tirade.

She didn't need to justify herself to Gina. She knew in her heart Suzy wasn't the culprit, and she was determined to clear her friend's name.

⚜ ⚜ ⚜

Once at the cottage, Lacey set Suzy up with a cup of tea and plate of buttered toast. They sat at the kitchen table, a reclaimed butcher's block made of light colored beech wood and silver metal brackets.

"Your house is so cool," Suzy said through her mouthful. "But I'd expect no less." She smiled, but the emotion didn't reach her eyes.

Lacey could tell she was using small talk as a diversion tactic, or a mask for her awkwardness over the whole situation. She'd probably had to go over and over the events of the night before with the police so many times the last thing she wanted to do now was talk about it again.

But Lacey had questions, and she needed answers. If she didn't solve this soon she'd have to declare bankruptcy. She'd lose her business, her home, she may even have to leave Wilfordshire altogether and go back to New York City with her tail between her legs. What would that mean for her relationship with Tom? And what about Chester? Would she even be able to take him with her?

"What happened last night, Suzy?" Lacey asked, managing to find her compassionate voice despite the rising panic fluttering in her chest.

Suzy put her toast down on her plate. Her bottom lip started trembling. "All I remember was the lights going out, the bang of the fireworks, and then a much louder bang that hurt my ears. Next thing I know, the gun was in my arms and Mayor Fletcher was ... was ..." A wave of tears overcame her.

"I'm sorry to make you go over this all again," Lacey said. "But it's important I understand what happened. Why were you in the drawing room in the first place, rather than out watching the fireworks with everyone else?"

"Honestly, I'd had about enough of Greg as I could stand," Suzy said. "I knew the firework display was his pride and joy moment, and I just decided to step away. That's all."

"So the others were already in there when you went in?"

She nodded. "Uncle Adrian and Mayor Fletcher were talking and drinking whisky by the bar. Ivan, Carol, and my aunt were by the fireplace."

"Right beside where the gun was mounted," Lacey noted, picturing it in its place above the mantel.

Suzy nodded slowly.

"So no one was holding it before the lights went out?" Lacey asked. "No one had taken it down to show it off or inspect it or anything?"

"No. It was right where it was meant to be."

"And it didn't look like it had been tampered with?"

Suzy frowned. "Tampered with? In what way?"

"Someone loaded the gun," Lacey explained. "It wasn't loaded when I brought it to the B&B and mounted it. Xavier confirmed it. So someone who had access to the rifle between me bringing it to the B&B and it being fired on Friday evening must have loaded it."

Suzy looked stunned. The half-eaten toast on her plate had been forgotten. Her tea remained untouched. "But if someone loaded it, then does that mean the murder was planned?" Her voice was going up in pitch as the horrible realization dawned on her, that it hadn't just been some horrible accident, but cold-blooded murder. "Do you think it was premeditated? A set-up? And the lights—was that planned too?"

She seemed gripped with sudden panic, and Lacey felt her stomach squirm. She had not wanted to tell Suzy that it had been her own clumsiness that had given the killer the opportunity to strike in such a brazen manner, but there was no getting round it. She was obviously distressed enough as it was that someone loaded the rifle in order to murder Mayor Fletcher; the last thing she needed was to think the lights had been deliberately cut as well, in order to carry it out.

"Actually, that was me," Lacey said. "I was chasing after Chester and I tripped. I must've tripped on one of the extension cables."

But Suzy's response to Lacey's explanation was to start shaking her head. "The cable was taped to the floor, with plastic protectors over them. Greg went on and one about how annoying it was that he'd have to put in all these extra safety measures because if one of my rich guests hurt themselves on it, he'd get sued. He even said, 'If there were only poor people coming, I wouldn't bother.' That's why I remember it so clearly, because it was such an awful thing to say. And besides, the cable was for the sound system, not the lights. Someone must've cut the lights purposefully, Lacey. Whoever wanted the mayor dead was devious."

Lacey let the information sink in. She hadn't been the one to trip the lights. Something else had turned them off.

The guilt she'd been carrying began to lift. But it didn't make her feel any better. Because Suzy was right. If the lights had been deliberately shut off, then the murder had been meticulously planned.

Someone had decided to murder the most important man in Wilfordshire right under the noses of the whole town, on the eve of the most important tourist day of the month, while they were gathered together celebrating a new chapter in the town's history. That opened up a frightening possibility to Lacey; that the mayor was targeted symbolically. To send a message.

Such a brazen, devious person like that would be very, very dangerous indeed.

Chapter Thirteen

Lacey fetched a spare set of pajamas, then showed Suzy up to the guest room. She'd offered Suzy her own bed, but Suzy had insisted on being the least of an imposition as possible.

"I hope you're able to nap with all those planes going past," Lacey said, as the buzz of a fleet passed overhead. It had been constant for hours now. Brits really did love an air show.

"I didn't sleep a wink at the station," Suzy said, diving under the duvet. "I doubt even the Red Arrows barrel rolling overhead could wake me."

"Well, don't oversleep and miss your check-in," Lacey said, setting the alarm clock for four hours' time, to give Suzy some leeway to get to the station. She turned up the volume to be extra sure.

"I won't. Thanks, Lacey. For taking really good care of me. For believing me ..."

Suzy looked like a child, with the cover pulled up to her chin, and her big brown eyes filled with nervousness.

Lacey smiled, but she knew she was doing it as much for herself as for Suzy. If Suzy missed her check-in time with the police, she'd be re-arrested. The longer she spent behind bars, the more time the rumor mill had to churn, and that might mean Suzy carrying the stigma of a murderer around with her forever. Her business would never get off the ground with a tarnished reputation, and that would have a huge knock-on impact with Lacey.

Lacey went over to the window and pulled the curtains tightly shut to block out the daylight. She'd invested in blackout blinds on Naomi's advice. Her sister had been going through one of her phases, this time all about increasing productivity by adopting a strange sleep pattern, and while Lacey had no desire to shorten her sleeping hours to four, she did think some of the advice for a good night's sleep was worthy, one being the importance of total darkness.

But as she drew the curtains for Suzy, a thought occurred to Lacey from the night of the murder. When she'd entered the drawing room, it had been in total darkness. But the fireworks display was still going on out in the garden. Lacey knew from her pursuit of Chester that the fireworks were bright enough to reach the corridor all the way from the patio doors in the dining room, which was a much bigger space than the drawing room, so subject to the weakening effects of light dispersal. So if the drawing room wasn't being lit by fireworks at the time of the murder, that could only mean the curtains were completely drawn. The thick velvet curtains Lacey had bought for the drawing room would certainly act as pretty good blackout blinds. Could the murderer have drawn them on purpose?

"Suzy," Lacey asked, swirling to face her, about to ask if she recalled anyone drawing the curtains. But the young woman was fast asleep, even snoring. Lacey turned to Chester instead. "I guess it's just you and me, boy. Fancy doing some sleuthing?"

Chester wagged his tail in affirmation.

❧ ❧ ❧

Where are you??

Lacey saw the message from Gina flash up on her phone's screen, which was lying on the dashboard of her Volvo, the other side of her steering wheel. Gina would have to wait. She had some serious sleuthing to do.

She'd parked down the tree-lined service road—knowing full well there would be a couple of police vehicles in the Lodge's parking lot she'd need to avoid. Getting in the Lodge was going to be a whole other issue she'd tackle when the time came. For now, just not being spotted on her approach was her goal.

She reached the turning into the side parking lot which connected to the B&B's kitchen. There were no vehicles, but the lurid blue and yellow police tape was cordoning off both the side sliding doors and kitchen emergency exits. Getting in through any of them would be risky.

Scanning the back of the property and drawing on her memory of the architect's schematics, Lacey determined that the best chance of actually making it inside undetected would be through the office window; it was just enough large enough for a woman of her size and a dog to enter through, and it had only a flimsy catch holding it closed.

She looked down at Chester by her feet and put a finger to her lips. "Quiet. Okay?"

His eyebrows twitched upwards in response.

Together, they skirted along the hedges that ran the length of the delivery lot, concealing it from public view. Birds started to twitter angrily as they disturbed their nests in passing, but luckily the sound of twittering birds was common enough in England that Lacey knew it wouldn't draw the attention of any police officers nearby.

Lacey reached the outer wall beside the office window, pressing her back against the bricks. She gestured to her ankles, in the gesture Chester knew meant he needed to heel. He obeyed her immediately and sat there looking up at her for his next command. This was all a fun game to Chester, Lacey thought. But for her, the high stakes of essentially breaking and entering a crime scene were rather anxiety inducing.

She took a quick peep through the window. Inside, the office was empty and in darkness. There was no sign of police tape like that cordoning off the outer doors. Hopefully, the police had not considered the window to be a viable entry point—from inside the office, the window looked like it was quite high, after all, and only someone with a detailed knowledge of the Lodge's layout would know there was a hillock on the other side.

Steeling herself, Lacey gripped the outer sash frame with her hands and gave it a small yank upwards. Through the glass, she saw the burnished gold latch quiver from the motion, before settling back into place. She tried again, putting more effort in this time, and the latch shifted. One more yank ought to do it.

Lacey heaved. The latch resisted her efforts, but finally it pinged off and the sash window slid upward so fast it bumped right into the top frame.

Lacey froze, straining to hear if anyone had been alerted to the noise. She heard no sound, no movement from inside. The coast was clear.

She looked at Chester and tipped her head to the side to indicate for him to go through the window. He did as she commanded, hopping down onto the desk under the window with the grace of an ibex. Lacey slipped inside after him, landing less gracefully on the desk, before hopping down to the floor.

She listened again, trying to hear if her intrusion had alerted anyone. Everything was quiet.

She went over to the office door and poked her head into the corridor, taking in the sight of the large reception desk in the middle, and a pool of light coming from the glass doors of the foyer, the place where any police officer would presumably be standing. There was only one thing for it. Run.

Lacey looked down at Chester and gave him the hand gesture to run, then pointed toward the drawing room door to indicate where. Immediately, he streaked off across the corridor and disappeared in through the door.

Lacey paused, watching, waiting to see if anyone had spotted him. Again, everything was quiet. She took her chances and ran for it.

Her heart was pounding in her ears as she bustled into the drawing room and shut the door behind her, leaning her back against it to catch her breath. Chester came up to her and fussed around her legs. She petted him.

"You did a good job, boy," she whispered.

Once she'd finally caught her breath, Lacey straightened up and paced further into the dim drawing room, her mind suddenly conjuring a whole host of questions that needed to be answered.

The first being, how did the killer aim in the dark? They'd have to be pretty confident in their shooting abilities to commit a murder blind.

She looked over at the curtains ... if the killer closed them, maybe they left fingerprints?

She paced over to get a closer look at the curtains. They were made of real velvet, which had a tendency to leave an imprint when accidentally pushed in the wrong direction. Maybe the killer had left their fingers imprinted in the fabric.

They were still drawn, clearly having been left untouched since the murder. It wasn't easy to see with the daylight blocked out and only low lighting coming from the lamps, and Lacey didn't want to touch them at all. She bent down and peered. But there was no sign of finger marks visible against the velvet.

Maybe the killer wasn't the one who closed the curtains? Lacey considered.

Only someone with an Olympic-level talent for shooting would choose such a risky set-up. But then ... only someone with very good knowledge of guns would have been able to load it in the first place.

Lacey had a sudden thought. They weren't dealing with a modern rifle here. The flintlock was an antique. It didn't just require knowledge, it required *historic* knowledge. The killer wasn't just adept at shooting, they were a gun enthusiast. A full on gun geek.

Perhaps if she dug into the backgrounds of her five suspects she'd find some clues?

The other thing Lacey was curious about was the lighting situation. Suzy was adamant Lacey hadn't tripped on the cable and caused it to come loose. She also said that the cable was for the sound system anyway, not the lights, but Lacey wasn't about to just take her word on that. Suzy wasn't always aware of Grumpy Greg's dealings in the B&B. If he could sneak a Spitfire on the posters, he could certainly have switched what cables powered what things without Suzy even knowing.

She went out into the corridor and peered beneath the rug runner that stretched the length of the corridor. Sure enough, the cable was concealed under a plastic sheeting. It wasn't exposed at all. There was no way Lacey could have tripped on it.

She followed the cable along its path into the garden, seeing it plugged in to the speakers that had been left, abandoned, since they were technically part of a crime scene.

Then just to be certain, Lacey traced the cable all the way back. Sure enough, it went into the dining room, into a socket concealed behind the bookcase.

She was certain now. The power was turned off. Deliberately.

But if the killer was in the room, preparing to shoot the mayor, then how did they turn the lights off?

Just then, Lacey heard the sound of footsteps clipping on the wooden floorboards in the corridor. Someone else was in the B&B! And by the sounds of it, they were heading right this way!

Lacey looked at Chester, filled with panic, and put a finger to her lips.

Then, glancing around, she leapt for the first appropriate hiding space; behind one of the long leather couches.

She thudded against the hard wooden floorboards at the exact same time she heard the door click open. Then she realized, with horror, that Chester hadn't followed her.

Of course he'd not understood that he was supposed to. He was so smart, Lacey sometimes forgot he was a dog.

She stole a glance around the side of the couch. Chester was sitting in the middle of the drawing room, his head tipped to the size in the way he did when he was puzzled.

There, standing in the door, was a figure.

They were pointing a gun right at Chester.

CHAPTER FOURTEEN

"No!" Lacey screamed, running out from her hiding place and waving her arms.

"Police! Freeze!" came the commanding voice of DCI Beth Lewis.

Lacey froze. Her heart leapt into her throat. She raised her hands above her head. "Don't shoot! Please don't shoot my dog!"

"Lacey?" DCI Lewis said, lowering her weapon and returning it to the concealed holster at her hip. "What are you doing here? You're trespassing. I should arrest you."

Lacey let her hands fall to her sides. Her racing heart began to slow.

"Should?" she asked hopefully. "Does that mean there's a chance you won't?"

She thought back to the station, To the triumphant moment they'd shared.

"You and Superintendent Turner are at loggerheads," Lacey said. Her use of the English term "loggerheads" slipped out almost without thought, as if Lacey was becoming more and more of a native speaker. "Again. He thinks Suzy did it and you know she didn't."

Beth remained silent, her expression unreadable. "Let me give you a bit of advice, Lacey. It's extremely common for killers to return to the scene of their crime. More often than not, we have the place under surveillance. So next time you decide to play amateur detective, be careful. If that had been any of the lads, you'd have earned yourself a chest full of lead. The males of our species tend to be a bit shoot first, ask questions later."

"Trust me, I've no intention of doing this ever again," Lacey said. "But I take your point. Speaking of the males of the species, was I right about Superintendent Turner? That you're at loggerheads with him over the case?"

Beth seemed hesitant to divulge anything about the case. She often was at first, Lacey reminded herself. Sooner or later, it would all come tumbling out. Because the detective knew Lacey was more likely to be reading from the same hymn sheet as her, unlike her bully of a supervisor.

"He thinks it's an open and shut case against Suzy," DCI Lewis said finally. "He's completely blinkered."

Sooner, Lacey thought. Aloud, she said, "He didn't okay you coming here, did he?"

The line appeared on Beth's lips again. "No. He didn't. I'm here on my own volition." She let a few beats pass. "What are your thoughts?"

"I think the killer planned this pretty meticulously," Lacey said. She started pacing, aware of the way Beth Lewis was following her intently with her eyes. "They chose to strike in conditions that would hide their crime in plain sight. They deliberately attempted to make the investigation confusing. The party setting meant a ton of unreliable witnesses with statements that didn't match up, people running all over the place, DNA shed here, there and everywhere. There's fireworks to lure everyone into the garden, and give the perfect cover for the sound of a gunshot." She snapped her fingers. "They chose this room in advance. We know that, because they'd already closed the curtains to stop anyone seeing in and to make sure if anyone happened to be in the room, they didn't see anything either."

She stopped pacing, her foot landing on a bulge in the rug beneath which the extension cord lay.

"Wait..." Lacey said, a new thought suddenly coming to her. The lights weren't knocked out because of her tripping on a cable. But the drawing room was lit by a myriad of antique lamps—quite an exquisite collection, Lacey couldn't help but note. Flicking the light switch wouldn't have plunged the room into darkness, but there was no way every lamp could have been switched off at the same time. The electricity had been cut via the fuses.

"There was an accomplice. The killer couldn't be in two places at once. Someone else cut the lights for them."

Beth nodded. "My observation exactly." Her expression remained as blank as always, but Lacey certainly felt a proud vibe ebbing from her. "Who amongst the five is your most likely suspect?"

"Right now, none," Lacey said. "But whoever has shooting skills would be top of my list."

"Because they made the shot in the dark."

"And because of the weapon they used."

Beth frowned, as if this was new to her. "What do you mean?"

"That's an 1820s original flintlock hunting rifle. It's an antique. The gun wasn't loaded when it was mounted. It didn't even have any ammunition. Only someone with expert knowledge would've been able to load that gun, or even know what ammo to use and where to buy it."

Immediately, Lacey stopped speaking and pressed her lips together. There had been one person in the room at the time of the murder with the knowledge of what ammo the gun took and where to source it. Lacey herself. The registered owner of the weapon. The person with the gun license, with the trading certificate...

There were no witnesses beyond the five in the room to corroborate her story that she was outside of the drawing room when the gun was fired. But the five inside the room were in total darkness. And Chester had run inside, hadn't he? Maybe one of them had heard him come in, blind and unable to identify the noise as a dog, and had told the police another person entered.

What if Beth was double-crossing her? Pretending they had some kind of affinity in order to get her to blab.

"That's interesting," the officer said. "I'll follow that up. And if you have any more interesting insights, let me know, okay? Me, not Karl." She handed her card.

"Will do," Lacey said, taking it.

But deep inside she couldn't help but think she was a suspect in this crime.

❧ ❧ ❧

Dusk was falling as Lacey returned home. When she got there, there was no sign of Suzy. She wondered if she was at the station, but her check-in would've been an hour earlier and should be over by now.

She heard Chester barking from the kitchen and went down, to find him beside the stable doors. She went out and found Gina and Suzy sitting together on the fold-out patio chairs overlooking the ocean and the beautiful sunset.

Lacey was surprised to see them together. Just a few hours earlier, Gina had insinuated that letting dangerous Suzy inside her house was the actions of a crazy person.

Lacey pulled up a third chair and sat beside them. "What are you two up to?"

They looked over at her. Both of them were holding cocktails. A jug of pinkish-looking liquid sat between them.

"Lacey!" Suzy exclaimed. She seemed to be in great spirits. "And look, it's Chester."

She ruffled the dog. Clearly the Dutch courage from the liquor had vanquished her phobia. Lacey was the same with spiders. If she came across one with alcohol in her bloodstream, it was under a glass tumbler and thrown into the garden; if she came across one stone cold sober, it ended up squished under the closest heavy object.

"We're watching the air show wind down," Gina said. "Would you like a drink? You've obviously been very busy today."

She'd used a pointed tone, and Lacey gasped as she suddenly realized she'd left Gina at the store all day, alone.

"I didn't come in to work!" she stammered.

"No," Gina replied, thinly. But she obviously wasn't too mad because she poured Lacey a cocktail.

"I invited Gina over," Suzy said. "I hope that's okay?"

"We bumped into each other on the high street. Suzy was on her way back from her station check-in, and I'd just locked up the store."

"And now you're tipsy."

"It is the weekend," Gina said.

Lacey settled down with her cocktail and sunset view. If Gina had been won around by Suzy, then Lacey was even more confident Suzy wasn't involved in Mayor Fletcher's murder. Her resolve to keep her out of jail strengthened.

Just as long as she could keep herself out at the same time.

CHAPTER FIFTEEN

T he house was quiet when Lacey awoke the next morning.
She passed by the spare room and could hear Suzy snoring loudly inside—sleeping off her pink cocktail–induced hangover, no doubt. Lacey decided it was best to let her sleep in for a little longer, so she headed downstairs to get her essential morning caffeine fix.

Chester trotted along beside her into the kitchen, sticking close by as she groggily stumbled through her morning routine: putting the coffee on to brew, pouring him a bowl of kibble, searching desperately for a clean mug, washing up random bits of cutlery that seemed to magically dirty themselves overnight. Today, there was a whole table's worth of grubby items from Gina and Suzy's evening of cocktail making. With a sigh, Lacey collected all the bits strewn around the place and dumped them in the farmhouse-style sink.

"I see you," Lacey said, narrowing her eyes as she noticed an offending spoon still lying on the dresser shelf.

She went over to the rustic floor-to-ceiling dresser—one of her favorite pieces in the whole cottage—and collected the sticky spoon. But as she did, she noticed the notepad she and Tom had been writing their suspect list upon was lying on the shelf, right beside the spoon, in full view of anyone.

What's that doing there? Lacey thought nervously.

What if Suzy had seen it? Her name was right there on the list, beneath Tom's crass title, "The Drawing Room Five"! With everything the poor girl was going through right now, the last thing she needed was to think her host was suspicious of her. It would be profoundly painful, Lacey imagined.

Luckily, the top page was covered in games of tic-tac-toe. Suzy and Gina must have been playing it last night during their evening of fun.

That was a close call, Lacey thought.

She picked up the notebook and leafed through the pages to the suspect list. Her gaze went immediately to Carol's name. It had been circled three times by Tom in black pen.

"Carol..." she said under her breath.

Of everyone on the list, the B&B owner was the one with the most obvious grudge against Mayor Fletcher. But then again, Carol seemed to take it in turns to hold a grudge against every resident of Wilfordshire. She was infamous for causing a ruckus in the weekly town meetings, and starting petitions if she didn't get her way. But if there was always someone Carol was mad at, would this specific grudge really have compelled her to commit murder?

From his place beside Lacey's legs, Chester whined.

"I know," Lacey said. "Something doesn't feel right."

Still mulling it over in her mind, she tugged open the drawer to tidy the notepad away again. But then something red caught her eye. Red pen.

Red? Red? Lacey thought frantically. *But that means someone else has written on it!*

She tensed as she quickly scanned the rest of Tom's notes. There, right beside Suzy's name (which Tom had left blank before), there was now a notation. In shaky red pen (which immediately made Lacey think of ransom notes written in blood) someone had added the words: *holding the smoking gun.*

Lacey swallowed hard.

Suzy must have added the note; Lacey could recognize Tom and Gina's handwriting. But why? Why add that?

"Morning," came Suzy's voice suddenly.

Lacey jumped and swirled around, hiding the notepad behind her back. Her heart leapt into her throat as she faced the young woman who'd appeared in the doorway like a phantom.

"You scared me," Lacey said, placing a hand to her fluttering chest.

Suzy stretched and let out a yawn. "Sorry. My parents always complained that I crept around the house like a ghost. I told them thirteen years of ballet lessons will have that effect." She sniffed the air. "Thought I smelled coffee. May I?"

She seemed chipper, Lacey thought, for someone nursing a hangover, and whose only means of income was under police seizure. Oh, and who was currently implicated in the murder of the mayor.

"I'll get it," Lacey told her.

She dropped the notebook into the open dresser drawer behind her, then pushed it shut with her backside and went over to the coffee machine.

Out the corner of her eye, Lacey couldn't help noticing the way Suzy was affectionately petting Chester's head without a care in the world. So it hadn't just been the Dutch courage pacifying her phobia last night; she really wasn't scared of dogs anymore. Along with the red note she'd added beside her own name, Lacey couldn't help but find it all rather suspicious.

"So what are your plans for this fine Sunday morning?" Suzy asked, now suddenly beside her at the window.

Lacey flinched, almost spilling coffee onto her hand. Suzy didn't seem to notice. She finished pouring her a mug, then handed it across to her.

"The usual," she said, cautiously, keeping her focus on pouring a second steaming mug for herself. "I'll take Chester for a walk along the beach into town, then open up the store for the day." She pictured her suspect list lying in the drawer, with Carol's name circled in black pen three times. "I'm planning on making some social calls, too." She finally looked over at Suzy, glancing over the lip of her coffee mug as she sipped it, making the eye contact she'd been avoiding this whole time. "You? What time are you supposed to check in at the police station?"

Suzy rolled her eyes, as if the fact her freedom had only come about on the proviso she checked in at the station every six hours was some trivial annoyance, rather than something significant.

"Eight AM," she said. "After that I'm having a phone conference with my parents and our solicitor." She sounded totally over it. "As you can imagine, they're pissed at me."

Lacey regarded her cautiously, leaning gingerly against the work surface, exuding a blasé attitude. None of it sat right with Lacey. But Chester was as content as could be in Suzy's company, and he was usually a very good judge of character. If he wasn't picking up vibes from her, then surely there were none there. Lacey was just being extra paranoid because of what had happened before with Brooke.

Just then, Suzy's gaze went over Lacey's shoulder and out the window. Her mouth dropped open. "You've got to be kidding me..."

Lacey turned to see what had prompted the reaction. An airplane was gliding through the cloudless blue sky.

"I thought the air show was over," Lacey began to say, before her voice trailed off as she realized the plane wasn't part of the air show at all. It was a private Cessna trailing an advertisement banner behind it. Bright pink words emblazoned across the banner read: *Carol's B&B – accommodation you can TRUST.*

Suzy thunked her coffee cup down onto the counter.

"How dare she!" she exclaimed. "Carol's really going to try and capitalize on the Lodge's closure?"

"Oh, Suzy," Lacey said, "I'm so sorry. That's just what she's like..."

"Cruel?" Suzy asked passionately. "Cold?"

"I was going to say opportunistic."

But cold was a good choice of word. It *was* a cold move. The sort of cold move one might expect from a cold-blooded killer.

Lacey plonked her coffee cup on the counter beside Suzy's with sudden determination. Her suspicions of Suzy were entirely unfounded. She was just on edge because of the far more obvious suspect staring her right in the face.

She looked back out at the banner fluttering in the sky. It was time to question Carol.

⚜ ⚜ ⚜

Lacey stepped through the doors into the familiar bubblegum-pink foyer of Carol's B&B. Carmella, the pretty Hispanic receptionist, was sitting at the reception desk in her clashing bright red uniform, a flower tucked in her shiny black hair.

She spotted Chester right away and put down her nail file. "You can't bring dogs in ... Oh, it's you!"

Her eyes had roved from Chester to Lacey. She obviously recognized her from the time she'd been trying to figure out who killed Buck when he'd been a guest at the B&B.

"I was wondering if—" Lacey began, but Carmella cut her off.

"Ohmygod," she said all in one breath. "Are you investigating Mayor Fletcher's murder?"

Apparently, Carmella thought Lacey was an actual detective, an illusion Lacey was in no hurry to shatter.

"Yes, that's right," she said, channeling her best Beth Lewis impression, by shoving her hands deeply into her pockets. "Is Carol—?"

She was interrupted again by Carmella. "Do you have any suspects? How was he killed? Was it mafia execution style? 'Cos I have this whole theory that he owed someone money. Either that or it was an ex-lover out for revenge."

Lacey regarded the over-excitable young woman. She had been just as crass when Buck had died, she recalled, as if she thought this was a reality TV show she got to be at the center of. But Lacey had to give her some leeway; she was young and foolish, she didn't yet fully comprehend the sanctity of life.

"Is Carol here?" Lacey asked, ignoring her questions in much the same way the detectives always did with hers.

Carmella shook her head. "She's at the police station, isn't she?"

"Yes, of course," Lacey replied.

Now that gave her pause for thought. If Carol, her preliminary prime suspect, was at the police station for further questioning, then that probably meant she was Beth Lewis's preliminary prime suspect, too. Lacey wasn't sure if she should feel reassured or not. On one hand, it was a relief to know that *she* wasn't top of the detective's list, but on the other hand, it meant the police were already one step ahead of her. If Superintendent Turner was as biased against Suzy as DCI Lewis seemed to think he was, how long would it take before he found a way to steer the trail back toward her?

Just then, Lacey realized that Carmella had started talking again. She tuned in.

"I know Carol can be a pain in the backside sometimes, but she's not a murderer, and I will totally give a character reference in court if you need me to."

I'm sure you would, Lacey thought, wryly, just picturing the girl on the stand lapping up everyone's attention.

"And I know she said she was going to get revenge but I'm sure that wasn't what she meant! And I guess someone got there first because *POW!*" She made a shooting gesture with her fingers. "The mayor was dead before she even got a chance."

Lacey winced. But before she could ask Carmella what she meant about Carol going to the party "to get revenge," a couple appeared at the flight of stairs—guests, obviously coming down for breakfast. They looked disturbed by Carmella's dramatic shooting gesture. Carmella herself looked a little embarrassed to have been caught doing it.

She hopped off her stool, her eyes falling to her feet sheepishly. "Let me show you to the dining room," she said, switching into hospitality mode.

As she guided the couple away, she glanced back over her shoulder at Lacey and flashed her a parting smile. Then she was gone.

Lacey stood in the pink foyer of Carol's, mulling over what the receptionist had just accidentally revealed to her.

"Revenge?" she said to Chester. "What does that mean?"

Chester tipped his head to the side and whined.

Lacey cast her mind back to the night of the party. When she'd first bumped into Carol by the water fountain, she'd startled her. And yes, she remembered now the look on her face, like Lacey had caught her in the middle of some sort of ploy. She'd definitely been up to something. But what? Murder?

And if Carmella was telling the truth about Carol going to the party "to get revenge," then she must've already known the mayor was there. But she'd acted like it was all news to her when Lacey had mentioned his name. She'd played dumb. Why? To throw Lacey off the scent? But then why be so stupid as to tell notorious blabbermouth Carmella of all people?

There were a lot of questions to untangle, and Lacey knew she wouldn't find any answers standing in the Barbie-pink hallway. Besides, its bright silliness suddenly felt oppressive.

"Come on Chester, let's go," Lacey said, shuddering with discomfort.

As she hurried back out of the door, she pictured the notepad and Carol's name circled three times. She mentally drew a fourth black circle around it.

Carol was still suspect number one. If anything, she was more of a suspect than before, because now Lacey knew she'd gone to the party specifically for revenge.

She wondered how long she'd be at the station for. Lacey needed to speak to her ASAP. But she got the distinct feeling she and Detective Lewis were going to be on one another's tails for the whole investigation.

If Lacey wanted to solve this, she was going to have to find a way to get ahead.

Chapter Sixteen

Thanks to Lacey's detour that morning via Carol's B&B, she was now late to open the store. Gina would be mad. She was always grumpy when she had to open the store alone, and would be especially so on a hangover day.

Lacey hurried along the cobblestone pavement with Chester trotting beside her.

But she'd not even made it past ten stores when she slammed straight into a man hurrying the other direction.

"Oof!" she exclaimed, almost knocked off her feet.

The man dropped the newspaper he'd been holding, and Chester barked at it as it slapped against the ground.

There, stark on the front page, was the smiling face of Mayor Bill Fletcher. The headline beside him read: MAYOR MURDERED?

Lacey bent down to pick up the newspaper. But at the same time, the man crouched down to do the same. They bumped heads.

"Will you be careful!" the man said gruffly, snatching the paper clean out of Lacey's hands.

Lacey instantly recognized his voice. "Ivan?"

The man's eyes darted up to meet hers. He looked so gaunt and pale she'd not even recognized him.

"Lacey?" he stammered. He'd always been timid and a little nervous, but it seemed even more pronounced today.

They both straightened to standing. Ivan tucked the paper under his arm, the mayor's face now obscured against his fleece sweater.

"Sorry for bumping into you," Lacey said. "I was rushing to get to the store. Where are you off to in such a hurry?"

She tried to sound conversational rather than nosy, but watched his reaction curiously. Ivan was one of the Drawing Room Five, so technically a suspect. She'd just given him no thought because of their personal connection, and the fact she couldn't imagine him being able to cause anyone physical harm. But here he was, standing before her like the shell of the man she knew, like someone who was hiding something...

"I'm going to get breakfast at the Coach House Inn," he said. "Catch up with the *Wilfordshire Weekly*. It's my Sunday tradition. Martha likes me out of the house for a couple of hours while she hosts her Sunday social mornings with the girls, so I have breakfast there, and then a roast at lunch."

"Sounds lovely," Lacey said. Then, quickly thinking on her feet, she added, "Mind if I join you?"

A brief flicker of agitation shone in his eyes. He rubbed the back of his neck. Clearly, the thought of having breakfast with Lacey did not appeal to him. Yet, Lacey knew he'd be far too polite to turn her away.

"Yes... uh... okay," Ivan stammered.

Lacey knew it had been a bit brash on her part to impose herself on him that way, but she would never solve the mayor's murder without speaking directly to the five people who'd been there when it happened.

They headed up the high street side by side, and silent. Lacey stole a quick glance at the window of her own store as she passed, catching sight of Gina bustling around dealing with the morning trade. She felt a pull to go inside. Chester also seemed to be automatically veering toward the store. But then Lacey caught sight of Mayor Fletcher's face peeking out from the crook of Ivan's arm.

Sorry, Gina, she thought. *I've got a murder to solve.*

⚜ ⚜ ⚜

"Two Full Englishes," Brenda the barmaid announced as she placed two plates down on the sticky wooden table.

With hungry anticipation, Lacey looked down at her plate of food. It was her first proper Full English breakfast experience (because although Tom had made her a home-cooked version once, he'd been careful to stress that poached eggs, sourdough bread, and farmer's market organic bacon were definitely not the norm). As she glanced down at the greasy, glistening sausages forming a dam between a lake of baked beans and the slightly gelatinous fried egg lying on top a stack of buttered white toast, she understood what he meant.

She slid her knife and fork out of the paper napkin they were wrapped in and poked the egg yolk. It split, sending gooey yellow yolk cascading against the other side of the sausage dam.

"Ketchup. Salt. And two ales," Brenda added, placing each item down as she announced it. "Enjoy." She turned and strolled away, hitching up her low – slung tracksuit bottoms as she did.

"Wow, she actually said 'enjoy," Lacey commented, as she sliced into her sausage. "I don't think Brenda's ever said anything pleasant to me before."

Not entirely sure how to approach the array of items on the plate in front of her, Lacey decided to take Ivan's lead. She copied him by dunking a sausage piece into the egg yolk, and scooping baked beans onto the rest of the available space on the fork. Then she watched him put the whole lot in his mouth in one go, braced herself, and did the same.

The food was definitely tastier than its appearance had led her to believe. Far from tasting greasy or oily, the flavors combined perfectly in her mouth. The meat, tangy beans, and creamy yolk hit different points of her palate, in a way her taste buds definitely approved.

"This is good," she murmured, covering her overly full mouth with her hand so as to avoid being impolite.

Ivan gave her a wane smile. Lacey immediately noted how the emotion didn't reach his eyes. He was clearly deeply troubled, and she was determined to get to the bottom of it.

"How are you?" Lacey asked him earnestly.

Ivan kept his eyes on his food. "I'm fine."

But he was far from fine and Lacey knew it. The stiff upper lip the Brits were so famed for wouldn't wash with her today.

"You're not," Lacey added. "I can tell."

Ivan squirmed in his seat. When he spoke again, his voice was low, barely a murmur. "I can't help thinking this is all my fault."

"Why would it be your fault?" Lacey asked, as a sense of disquiet washed over her.

Was Ivan about to admit to something? Surely he'd not had a hand in killing the mayor. He was far too gentle! Too honest. Kind to a fault.

But then, Lacey had witnessed firsthand his fit of rage when he'd realized the mayor was at the party. It had been out of character, and had shocked her to see him that way. But being roused to anger by the presence of the man who'd ruined your business was one thing; being roused into a murderous disposition was quite another. And Ivan didn't fit the rest of the culprit's profile—the killer Lacey was looking for must have premeditated the murder if they'd gone to the length of loading the gun. They were an experienced gunman. If Ivan *had* killed the mayor, it could only have been because of a sudden loss of control, a fit of repressed rage boiling over in a split second.

Or was she just making assumptions? Because really, how well did Lacey actually know Ivan Parry? Brooke had deceived her. Maybe Ivan's bumbling persona was all an act as well.

"Never mind," Ivan said, focusing his attention on his food.

His response did little to ease her now ruminating thoughts.

As she scooped gloopy orange beans onto her fork, Lacey cast her mind back to the party, to the moment the lights had come back on to reveal Mayor Fletcher lying injured on the floor. Ivan had tried to call an ambulance, on Councilor Muir's command, but had dropped his phone.

The memory repeated in her mind's eye, of the phone skidding across the floorboards, and Ivan making no attempt to retrieve it. At the time, Lacey had put the whole thing down to shock. But what if Ivan had staged his sudden butter fingers to make sure medical help wouldn't arrive in time to save Bill Fletcher's life?

Suddenly, Lacey's mind was turning at full speed. How much did she really know about the man carefully cutting up hash browns opposite her?

"I keep hearing it," he said suddenly, his eerie whisper breaking Lacey from her ruminations with a start.

She was surprised he was opening up to her, so she sat back, unobtrusively, and listened as he continued, his gaze unfocused on the middle distance.

"The bang. It was so loud. And that smell of gunpowder…" His eyes found hers, finally. "But it's the blackness that really gets me. It was so dark. I couldn't see anything at all and, you see, I've always been afraid of the dark."

Lacey regarded him with interest. "So what happened after the lights cut out?"

"I froze. Everyone else in the room let out a little 'oh!' noise, and then started to chuckle. Someone said something like, "power cut," or words to that effect. And then … BANG."

He closed his eyes, his expression somewhat tormented as he grappled with the memories.

"Did you hear anyone taking the gun off its mount?" Lacey asked.

Ivan had been right there, according to Suzy. Right beside the gun. If anyone was in a position to hear the perp in action, it was him.

He shook his head vehemently. "No. Nothing at all. The gun was there before the lights cut out. When they came back on, it was in Suzy's arms."

Lacey couldn't help but feel suspicious. Because whoever had taken the rifle down from its mounting on the wall would've had to have brushed right past him to get to it. If Ivan neither heard nor felt anyone passing him, could that be because it was Ivan himself who took the gun down?

"How's the food?" came the sudden voice of Brenda from beside them.

Lacey looked over to see the permanently bored-looking barmaid looming over her.

"It's lovely, thanks," she said, a little annoyed at being interrupted.

Brenda picked up the *Wilfordshire Weekly* from beside Ivan. "Who do you reckon will replace Mayor Fletcher?" she asked.

Lacey squirmed from her brazenness. Opposite her, Ivan swallowed hard, his eyes averted from the young woman who knew no better.

"I'm not sure anyone will want to put themselves forward," he said, quietly. "Considering the circumstances."

"What about that lady who stood last time?" Brenda asked. "Whatsername? I'd be up for a bit of Girl Power."

"Her name's Joan Muir," Ivan said, briskly. Then he coughed into his fist, as if realizing he'd been too curt.

Brenda shrugged, her interest in the topic obviously spent, and tossed the paper back onto the tabletop carelessly. Ivan neatened the paper as she walked away. The whole awkward exchange had left him looking even more flustered than before.

But Brenda's thoughtless questions had lit a spark in Lacey's mind.

"*Is* Joan going to run for mayor?" she asked.

"How would I know?" Ivan replied, sounding affronted.

"Oh. I'm sorry. I just thought because you worked on her campaign trail last time she might've mentioned she wanted to run again..."

"She has new advisors now," he snapped. "I don't know what they're telling her to do, but I know what my advice would be. Don't put on a dead man's shoes while they're still warm."

Lacey couldn't help but feel uncomfortable at his choice of words, even if it was just a metaphor. There was a very obvious undercurrent to Ivan's words, a scathing tone directed at her aides. He was obviously bitter about having been cast aside.

Lacey needed to get more out of him. But Ivan appeared to have become even more dejected throughout their conversation. There was only one other way. She would have to toy a little with the man's sensitive nature.

Naomi had taught her the crying trick many moons ago. "Just think about when your first pet died, and the tears will come instantly." Lacey did it now. She'd not had a pet as a kid growing up in the busy city of New York, but she'd been very fond of a goose in her local park. When it migrated for winter, she'd been heartbroken.

Sure enough, it worked. Lacey felt her eyes brim with tears.

"You know, I've been feeling super guilty over all of this," she said to Ivan, her eyes blurring as the hot tears filled them.

"You? But why?" the man said, kindly.

"The rifle belonged to me. It was my responsibility to make sure it was stored properly, and that it was sold in a safe condition." She lowered her voice, preparing for her first white lie. "I didn't realize it was against the law to sell it loaded. If the police find out, I'll go to prison."

As a fat tear plopped from her eye onto the table, Lacey studied Ivan's reaction. If he was the killer, he'd know Lacey hadn't sold the gun loaded because he would have had to have loaded it himself. So if he showed any signs of relief, she'd know it was because he'd been presented with an opportunity to pass the blame onto someone else.

He handed her one of the paper napkins the cutlery had been wrapped in. "It'll be all right," he said, tenderly. "I'm sure the police have far more important things to be concerned about than that. Like finding the murderer."

Lacey wasn't sure what to make of that. He didn't seem to have reacted to the bait at all. She'd have to try something different.

"Yes, I guess whoever fired the gun is more responsible," she sniffed, dabbing her eyes with the tissue. "I mean, they were obviously a very skilled shooter if they knew how to fire an antique weapon in the dark. It must have been someone very experienced."

This time, she noticed a change in Ivan's expression. It was a small change, but it was definitely there. A sort of flicker of understanding. She noticed his Adam's apple bob up and back down as he swallowed.

He stood suddenly, discarding his napkin onto the plate of food. "Sorry, Lacey, I've just remembered ... I have something to do."

He hurried away, leaving the napkin to soak up the bean juice of his half-eaten English breakfast.

Lacey watched him go with perplexed interest.

When she'd first bumped into him, he'd seemed perturbed. But now, he seemed more like he was haunted. Troubled. Burdened. Like he was carrying a secret.

Lacey's meeting with Ivan Parry had left her with more questions than answers.

CHAPTER SEVENTEEN

T he doorbell tinkled above her as Lacey attempted to sneak into the store unnoticed. No such luck.

"Look who's finally decided to join us!" Gina exclaimed.

Lacey looked up, sheepishly, and met her friend's eye. Chester shoved his way past her legs and went bounding over to greet Boudica with a wagging tail and sniffing nose. But their human counterparts exchanged a slightly less enthusiastic greeting.

"Sorry," Lacey said. "I wanted to do some sleuthing before I opened up this morning, but it ended up taking a bit longer than I'd anticipated. Have you been busy?"

Gina folded her arms. "Busy? Busy? What do you think! It's air show weekend! I've been rushed off my feet."

"I'm sorry," Lacey said again. "I'm here now."

She headed toward Gina behind the counter. But the store's bell tinkled before she made it, and Lacey turned around to face the customer who'd entered.

To her surprise, it was Carol standing in the doorway of the store. Her face was red and tear-stained.

"Lacey, can we talk?" Carol asked in an uncharacteristically small voice.

"Of course," Lacey said, taken aback.

Carol looked over at Gina. "Privately."

Lacey flashed Gina an apologetic smile (which was returned with a stern glare and narrowed eyes), before whisking Carol into the back office.

It felt like a million years had passed since Lacey had sat in the small, dark room, creating sketches and mood boards for the Lodge's decor. But it had only been a matter of days; her work was still strewn all over the place.

"Just shove that aside," Lacey said to Carol, who was glancing around for a seat that wasn't covered in papers. "Do you want coffee? Tea?"

Carol nodded. "Yes. That would be nice."

Lacey paused, kettle in hand. "Which one?"

"Oh. Sorry, Lacey. My mind is somewhere else. Tea. Thank you."

Lacey had never seen Carol like this. The woman was usually so self-assured, and sharp as a tack. To see her dithering and nervous was certainly curious.

Lacey made the tea and handed Carol a cup. Then they sat opposite one another, so close in the cramped office their knees were almost touching.

"I need to apologize," Carol blurted immediately, clasping her mug in both hands like it was a security blanket.

"Oh?" Lacey said.

"I've been rude to you," Carol said. "Terribly rude. And all this business with the mayor has made me realize how we should stick together. Because life is so fragile and it can get taken away from you in the blink of an eye. And I'd hate for you to have ill feelings toward me. Can it all be water under the bridge?"

Lacey didn't know what to make of the apology, nor of Carol's sudden meek mannerisms. She'd never seen the bulldozer of a woman look this way and it was disconcerting.

The apology, she suspected, was disingenuous. Carol was up to something. Maybe Carmella had told her about Lacey's visit to the B&B and she was here to head off Lacey's suspicions. Because why else would she be putting herself in the firing line of Lacey's questions like this?

Lacey decided to play the game and see what information she could squeeze out of the cunning Carol.

"Sure," she said, her gaze glued on Carol, studying her every move. "Water under the bridge."

Carol let out an exhalation, as if in relief. Then she coyly ran her fingers around the rim of her coffee cup. "So ... have the police been in touch with you at all?"

Her tone was innocent enough, but Lacey could immediately tell she was digging for something. Well, two could play that game.

"No," Lacey told her. "I'm sure they will though. They'll be working their way through the witnesses in order of interest."

Her attempt to put on the pressure worked. Carol immediately shifted uncomfortably in her seat. She must know that being given the first interview of the day meant she was the police's priority.

"Have you?" Lacey added.

"Oh yes, I've given my statement," Carol said hurriedly, evasively. "They had a lot of questions about ... the gun."

Her eyes flicked up, and Lacey could see she was regarding her just as cautiously as Lacey was regarding her. Either she was attempting to deflect attention, or she was just as suspicious of Lacey as Lacey was of her.

"Oh?" Lacey asked.

"Mmm," Carol replied with a nod. "They seem very interested in whether I had prior experience with shooting. Or whether I knew if the others did."

"Interesting," Lacey said, keeping her tone level. "And what did you tell them?"

"I don't know about the others, but *I* certainly don't. I mean, I was one of the original campaigners to get the shooting club shut down all those years ago!"

"Is that so?" Lacey said, her mind working at a mile a minute trying to decipher what exactly Carol's game was here.

"Yes, believe it or not, I was raised by hippies on a commune," Carol continued. "Strictly vegan lifestyle. I may have grown more lax in my old age, but I'm still the first on the picket line when the fox hunters roll into town."

Lacey narrowed her eyes suspiciously. She couldn't tell if Carol had sussed her out and was deliberately dropping in convoluted stories to make Lacey think she couldn't possibly be the culprit.

But as much as she wanted to carry on her investigation, she could help but think about the shooting club Carol had been instrumental in getting closed down. The shooting club her father might very well have secretly belonged to behind her mother's back.

"Do you remember much about the old shooting club?" she asked, curious now for herself rather than her investigation. "I know it operated from the old Penrose Estate hunting lodge."

"It closed. They said financial mismanagement but I'd like to take some credit. I spent a fair few summers chained to the oak tree out in their shooting field." She laughed with triumph.

Councilor Muir had said the same thing herself. Financial mismanagement. She wondered who was managing the finances at the time.

"Good riddance if you ask me," Carol said. "I was always saying that guns were too dangerous to have in our town. And now I've been proven right!"

Lacey was expecting a pointed glare from Carol then—as the inconsiderate outsider who'd brought a dangerous weapon into their peaceful community—but none came. Either she really did want to make amends, or she was doing her hardest to butter Lacey up and remove suspicion from herself.

Well, whatever game she was playing, Lacey wasn't going to passively let it pass her by. She was going to join in.

"Carol, what were you doing at the party on Friday? If you're a lifelong vegan, you weren't there for the grilled chicken, that's for sure. I know you were planning something." She stopped, not wanting to throw Carmella's name into the mix as her accidental blabbermouth source.

"I may as well come clean," Carol said, "since I already told the police everything. I was there for sabotage."

Lacey blinked, surprised. "I'm sorry, what?"

"Sabotage. I had a bottle of Fairy Liquid in my purse and I was going to dump the lot in the fountain when you were all outside. Bubbles galore. That was all. I wasn't there to murder the mayor, if that's what you're insinuating."

"Wait ..." Lacey said, something Carol had said sparking off a whole new line of thinking. "Fireworks. That would've been the only time when everyone was outside. But you weren't in the foyer with the fountain during the fireworks, you were in the drawing room."

"I have a rare condition," Carol said, without missing a beat. "Photosensitivity to certain lights. I went into the drawing room and closed the curtains so the flashes wouldn't bother me. I was going to wait until the show ended, then dump the liquid before any of you came back inside."

Lacey couldn't help but think it all sounded a bit farfetched. Carol seemed to have an answer for everything, and quite an elaborate one at that. Anti-gun protestor. Fairy Liquid saboteur. Photosensitive to fireworks. Had Carol come to this meeting with pre-prepared answers to any possible question she thought Lacey might bring up?

"You closed the curtains?" Lacey asked.

Carol nodded. "Yes. Why?"

Lacey shook her head. "Nothing."

She was more confused than ever.

From the shop floor, Lacey could hear the bell tinkling over and over, as yet more air show tourists came in.

"I'd better help Gina," she said. "She's been rushed off her feet."

Carol stood. "I hope we've cleared the air now, Lacey." She held her arms open. The last thing Lacey wanted to do was embrace the woman, but she did.

"Don't worry. Water under the bridge."

"Excellent," Carol said. "I'm so relieved we can go back to normal now. Us. The town. Everything's as it should be."

"Wait. What do you mean, the town?"

"Well, now the mayor's dead, that awful regeneration project's come to a halt. Didn't you hear? It's the silver lining in this whole debacle."

And with that, she left. Lacey watched her go, feeling cold all over.

Carol hadn't put her suspicions to rest at all. If anything, she'd made them a whole lot worse.

CHAPTER EIGHTEEN

"**I**'m sorry, but Councilor Muir is unavailable to speak to her constituents over the telephone," said the droll voice on the other end of the line. "If you want to raise a community question with her, she holds her drop-in surgeries on Wednesdays, or I can book you an appointment in a fortnight."

It took Lacey's mind a moment to realize the receptionist wasn't talking about *surgery* in the sense that she understood it—with a doctor and a scalpel—but was referring to the one-to-one meetings English councilors held with members of the public.

Lacey sighed, her fingers playing idly with the long cord of the vintage telephone. "This isn't a community-related question. It's regarding Bill Fletcher."

There was a muffled sound, like someone covering the speaker with their hand. A moment later, the voice asked, "Are you a reporter?"

Clearly someone was standing behind this hapless receptionist feeding them lines. "No. I already told you who I am. Councilor Muir knows me personally. I need to speak to her urgently."

There was another long pause while the receptionist acted as a go-between. It was enough to test Lacey's patience.

She looked down at Chester and rolled her eyes. He whinnied sympathetically.

A scritch-scratch noise through the speaker told Lacey the phone had been passed over to someone else, and now a new voice sounded in her ear.

"This is Benson, Councilor Muir's aide. She's unavailable to speak but I can relay a message to her."

This was useless. Lacey would never get to the information she needed if there was always an intermediary between her and Joan Muir. And she couldn't wait until Wednesday for a chance of a face-to-face meeting, especially since it wouldn't be a private one.

"Can you please just tell her Lacey needs to speak to her urgently."

"I will."

The call cut out before Lacey had a chance to pass on her contact details.

She slammed the receiver down with frustration.

"Well, that was a waste of time," she told Chester.

Although, speaking to Councilor Muir had become less of a priority now that Lacey had moved her to the bottom of the suspect list. After what she'd learned about Ivan, and what had been reaffirmed by her chat with Carol, Joan Muir had become a far less likely candidate. Unlike Ivan and Carol, she had no reason to want the mayor dead, and she also tried to save his life.

Just then, the bell over the door interrupted Lacey from her ruminations. She glanced up and saw a woman had entered—one of the regulars whose name Lacey didn't yet know.

The woman went straight to Chester, crouching down and patting his head.

Ah, yes, Lacey thought. *She's one of Wilfordshire's Chester-petters.*

The pup lapped up the attention. But when the woman stood again, Lacey saw she was crying.

"Oh. Is everything okay?" she asked.

The woman sniffed. "I'm fine," she said, shaking herself off. "Do you have any whisky memorabilia? Old bottles, preferably. I need them to put candles in. My husband was a whisky connoisseur and the children and I are going to have a family vigil."

Lacey connected the dots immediately. This was Bill Fletcher's widow.

Before Lacey had a chance to reply, Gina returned from her break and came round the back of the counter. She placed a copy of the *Wilfordshire Weekly* down on it, and a black-and-white Bill Fletcher grinned up at everyone.

Lacey reached for it in an attempt to turn it over. But it was already too late. Mayor Fletcher's widow saw it and burst into tears.

She ran out of the store in a flurry.

"What was that about?" Gina asked.

"That was Mrs. Fletcher. Bill's wife."

"Uh-oh," Gina said, looking guiltily at the paper. But then her eyes roved over to the notepaper Lacey had been scrawling notes on. She put her hands on her hips. "What's that?"

"Nothing," Lacey said. Now it was her turn to be guilty.

"You're still sleuthing, aren't you? Did you even stock up the teapot shelf?" She craned her head to check. "No. Of course not. And I suppose you've not logged the inventory of the box that was delivered earlier either, have you?"

Lacey gestured to it still sitting unopened behind her.

Gina shook her head. Then she held out her hand, palm up. "Give it here then. The notepad. Let me help."

Lacey didn't need telling twice. She handed it over, watching Gina's expression as she scanned all the information Lacey had already gathered.

"Interesting," she said. She tapped the notebook. "So what about this Adrian fellow? You've not contacted him."

"He's a tricky one," Lacey told her. "For starters, he was standing by the bar with Mayor Fletcher when he died. Which was the other side of the room from where the gun was."

"But was the blackout long enough for him to shove the gun into Suzy's arms then stroll over to the bar?"

"He was standing at the bar *before* the blackout, too. The only way he'd be able to get to the gun, shoot it, pass it to Suzy, then get back to his original spot again was if he was some kind of stealthy owl with night vision." She took the notepad from Gina and stared at it as if it were covered in indecipherable hieroglyphics. "Although Ivan said he didn't feel anyone pass him, and that could explain why. Adrian would have approached from the other side."

"Write it down," Gina said, nodding with her head at the notepad.

Lacey scribbled it down. But she wasn't convinced.

"Why would he shove the gun at Suzy?" she mused aloud. "She's his niece. He likes her enough to support her when her family had other commitments and couldn't come."

"Mistaken identity?" Gina said with a shrug. "He might've just shoved the gun at whoever was closest, not realizing it was Suzy until the lights came back. What was his behavior like after the fact?"

"He seemed ... unmoved," Lacey said, choosing her words carefully. But that was the best description. Out of everyone in that room, Uncle Adrian had seemed the least affected. "I put it down to shock. A bullet had literally just whizzed a few inches past him, after all."

"Shock, maybe," Gina replied, shrugging. "Or callousness. They look similar on the surface."

Lacey nodded her agreement. "Still, it doesn't explain how he could zip around the room so quickly."

"But who were the witnesses who placed him at the bar in the first place? The other four of the Drawing Room Five? Because let's not forget they'd just been plunged into sudden darkness, heard a gunshot, and were then confronted with a dying man bleeding out on the floor. How reliable are any of their memories, really?"

It was a good point.

"So I should follow up the uncle route," she said, tapping Adrian's name on her paper.

Gina plucked the notepad from her hand. "Actually, you should log the inventory from that delivery and restock the teapot shelf. I shouldn't need to keep reminding you that you have a store to run."

She had a real knack, Gina, of switching seamlessly from friend to surrogate mother.

"There won't be a store if I don't get this sorted soon," Lacey told her. "Because every day the B&B is closed is another day I'm not getting my invoice paid. Ivan might let me miss a house payment, but my credit card company sure as heck won't! They don't care about the extraneous circumstances. I need this done and dusted. So, if you wouldn't mind watching the store for a little while longer while I do some research on Uncle Adrian, I'd be most grateful?"

Gina did not look thrilled. She folded her arms.

"The garden!" Lacey exclaimed. "Just think about that massive garden at the Lodge. The one Suzy wants to hire you to tend. The longer the Lodge stays closed, the farther away that dream becomes."

Now she had her.

"Fine," Gina said. "You go and play detective. But I'm expecting a bonus after all these solo shifts I've been doing."

"If I can solve this," Lacey told her, "you'll be getting a bonus, a pay raise, and every cake in Tom's store."

But tracking down Uncle Adrian proved to be even more difficult than Councilor Muir. He wasn't listed in the phone book, and he appeared to be the only man in existence without an internet footprint. She was reluctant to ask Suzy as well, worried that the girl might be offended that she was even looking into him in the first place, since he'd have to be an acrobat to have crossed the room twice to carry out such a feat.

In her dark back office with no window, Lacey started to feel a little loopy.

"Maybe he's a doctor?" she said, typing *Doctor Adrian Rowe* to see if it yielded any hits.

No luck.

Maybe he's a professor.

She tried Professor Adrian Rowe. Then Lord Adrian Rowe. Then his Royal Highness Adrian Rowe. None brought her any closer to the man.

She was about to give up her futile search attempts, when she remembered something Suzy had mentioned during one of the many conversations that had taken place while they'd restored the B&B together. Suzy had mentioned a friendly sibling rivalry between her father and Uncle Adrian over a peerage, and Lacey hadn't really thought about what that meant at the time.

She typed Sir Adrian Rowe and hit return.

This time, she'd found him.

"Uncle Adrian is a Sir!" she exclaimed.

And it wasn't just that. As she scrolled through his information, she learned his entire career had been in the field of shooting.

The revelation sent Lacey into an immediate tailspin. Uncle Adrian would have known how to load the old gun. But he couldn't have zipped across the room so quickly. That meant one thing.

Was Adrian the accomplice?

CHAPTER NINETEEN

L acey spread the detail drawing of the Lodge's drawing room she'd sketched during the renovation work across the counter of the store. Gina had gone on a break to walk the pups, so Lacey grabbed the first spare moment within the lull of customers to continue her investigative work.

She stared down at the drawing, which was an almost perfect representation of how the room had eventually turned out, except Lacey had expected there to be a proper bar complete with optics in the corner instead of the mahogany sideboard that was repurposed for it instead, and there was no sign of the collection of brass coal shoots because Lacey had purchased them at the last minute.

She laid a piece of tracing paper over the image, grabbed a pencil, and added in the places where each individual had been standing at the time the lights turned back on. As her memory served, Uncle Adrian was standing beside the bar, closest to where Mayor Fletcher was lying. The other four had been clustered beside the fireplace; Carol closest to the door where Lacey stood, then Suzy, who was next to Councilor Muir, who was next to Ivan, who was closest of them all to Adrian, although there was a gap of several feet between them. On the paper, Lacey added various arrows from each person to the mayor to indicate possible trajectories of a gunshot. The end result was perplexing to say the least.

Just then, the store bell jingle-jangled and in stomped Taryn. She came up to the counter and slammed a piece of paper down in front of Lacey.

"And what's that?" Lacey asked.

"That is a letter from my electricity supplier," Taryn said. "Saying I can't switch companies because my meter has been locked into a contract with some stupid eco company. A company I most definitely did not switch to."

"Ah," Lacey said, realizing what had happened.

Several stores on the street shared their electricity boxes—because, Lacey had discovered, modern utilities in old English buildings were a hodgepodge mess at the best of times. The stop cock for her water supply was literally *under* the cobblestones outside, the original architects having clearly not considered such an event as a burst pipe, and the pipe was shared by several stores in the terrace, so if one was cut off, they all were. They also shared some other utilities—the gas pipe, internet cables—all the meters of which were collected together in a weird sort of underground bomb shelter–type structure located off the back footpath, which Lacey avoided entering at all costs since there were no lights and always at least one fat spider suspended on a web at eye level for her to walk face-first into. Even though she was supposed to submit monthly meter readings, Lacey usually chose to pay the higher estimated bill rather than enter the dark little hovel. Only this month, she'd been brave and had gone in with her flashlight to take down the serial numbers so she could switch suppliers to a renewable energy one. Evidently, she'd read the wrong one.

"You gave them the wrong meter number, didn't you?" Taryn accused.

"Sorry," Lacey said. "You know how dark it is in the basement. I'll..."

Her voice trailed off as her mind began to suddenly whirr.

"You'll what?" Taryn snapped, grabbing the bill from the counter. "You'll call the company and get me released from the contract? Refund me for the extra money I've had to spend on green wind turbine–generated electricity from Denmark?" She waved the paper around furiously.

"Yes, yes, yes," Lacey said, shooing Taryn away, not wanting to lose her train of thought.

Taryn glared at her, then with a huff, she spun on her heel and stomped toward the exit. "I want a refund on that ugly Edison lamp as well," she shouted as she heaved the door open. "I *hate* it!"

With that, she walked out, the bell tinkling angrily as she slammed the door behind her.

But Lacey had hardly heard a thing. Her mind had gone to the basements, and old English architectural peculiarities, meter boxes and fuses... A single tripped fuse could plunge half the street into darkness.

Lacey raced into the back office and rummaged through her interior design work, searching for the schematics for the Lodge. It had all the technical details, from the length of walls to the heights of doors, the placement of fire alarms to the depth of wall cavities. She flicked through the layers—exterior, attic, third floor, second floor, ground floor.

"There!" Lacey said, tapping the paper. Just past the corridor where the reception desk had been relocated was the door that led down to the basement, or *cellar* as the Brits called it.

She flipped the final page. The fuse boxes were right there, beside the foot of the stairs. Easy to reach for anyone coming into the basement.

"The accomplice tripped the fuses," Lacey said aloud.

Just then, Lacey heard the shop bell tinkle. She hurried out onto the shop floor to see Gina entering with Boudica and Chester in tow. Her cheeks were bright red and her gray hair was stuck to her brow with sweat.

"Blimey, it's hot today," she said, releasing the dogs from their leashes. They ran past her legs, clearly exuberant from their walk. "What the heck is wrong with Taryn? I just saw her marching into her store with a face like thunder."

"Some drama over a bill," Lacey said distractedly.

As the pups muzzled one another in an attempt to get the good snoozing spot, Lacey scooped her purse up and came around the counter onto the shop floor.

"I have to go and do something," she told Gina. "Do you mind—"

"—watching the store?" Gina finished for her, raising her eyebrows into an unimpressed expression. "I do, but I don't think that will stop you."

"I'm sorry," Lacey said, already hurrying for the exit. "I've just thought of a lead I need to pursue." She tugged open the door. "Just think of all that time I'll give you off to work on the B&B's garden once this is all over!"

She raced away, leaving Gina standing in the middle of the shop shaking her head.

Lacey hurried up the street to the side alley where her car was parked. Her mind was racing with a new line of thinking triggered by Taryn's hissy fit over the meter in the basement.

All the lights in the lodge went out in one go, not from her tripping over a cable, but by someone switching them off at the fuse. And where was the fuse box she'd just been looking at on the detail sketch? The basement! The basement whose door was in full view of the corridor.

She hadn't thought about how likely it would have been for the killer's accomplice to have been witnessed by someone at the party going into the basement. The basement door was just a little way past the large mahogany reception desk that cut the B&B's corridor in half, blocking guests from accidentally wandering into the kitchen or back rooms. It was in full view of anyone in the corridor. *Or* the kitchen.

"The caterers!" Lacey exclaimed.

A whole bunch had been drafted in for the night. They were the most likely out of anyone at the party to have seen someone enter the basement door from their vantage point *and* they wouldn't have been out in the garden during the fireworks display either, since they were busy working in the kitchen. Grumpy Greg had organized the temp staff himself, and Lacey thought it was highly unlikely he'd have allowed any one of them to break to watch the fireworks.

"Greg…" Lacey muttered, her stomach dropping. "Dammit."

It had just occurred to her what she would have to do, something she'd avoided doing at all costs as she'd worked on the decor in the B&B. Speak to Greg.

She reached her car, unlocked the driver's side, and slid into her seat. She took out her phone and quickly texted Suzy.

I have a lead. Can you send me Greg's number?

Lacey had made such a habit of avoiding the surly events planner during her work at the B&B, she hadn't even gotten his number, even though the two of them needed to coordinate some of their efforts.

Her phone pinged. Suzy had sent Greg's contact details, along with a message.

What do you want to speak to Greg for? I know he was difficult, but I don't think he had anything to do with this.

Lacey quickly typed back: *He's not a suspect, don't worry. I just think he might know something.*

She dialed the number Suzy had sent her, and the voice of Grumpy Greg sounded in her ear as he answered the call.

"Lacey from the B&B?" he asked, as soon as she'd introduced herself. "What do you want?"

Charming, Lacey thought but did not say. "I wanted to ask you about the night of the party. About the temp staff you hired."

"What do you want to know? And don't ask for their names. I was rushed off my feet all evening. I barely had time to breathe, let alone get to know the temps!"

Lacey couldn't help but roll her eyes at his over-the-top dramatics.

"Besides," he continued, "it would violate privacy law for me to hand out their details. If you need to hire them you'll have to go through the same agency—"

"Actually, I was just wondering if they had access to the basement at all?"

"Of course they didn't," Greg said, in the sort of tone that should be preceded by "you ignorant girl." "It was strictly off limits. Suzy had a whole load of Swiz wines stored down there sent by her parents, since they felt so guilty about missing the grand opening. I told her it was ludicrous to have them so far away from the wait staff, and she said that she only wanted people she trusted going down to the basement to fetch them. So if you're interested in the basement, you should probably ask that child about it."

"What child?"

"The horsey one. Lucy, was it? She was in and out of the basement all night."

Lacey froze. Did he mean Lucia?

Her mind began to race, combing through the events of Friday evening. She'd hardly seen Lucia at the party all night. Beyond that time she'd spotted her giggling away with Tom in the foyer, and being there in the garden at the beginning of the fireworks, she'd not run into her once.

But beyond a complete lack of motive, would Lucia even have had the time to come inside from the beginning of the fireworks display and shut off the lights? She would've had to have followed right in after Lacey to do it, then peel off through the adjoining dining room door and out through the kitchen to the basement door in the corridor. Yes... it was possible. But was it plausible?

Lacey realized Greg was still speaking. She turned her focus to his voice.

"I bumped into her at the YMCA extravaganza I went to at the weekend. The patisserie she works for was catering. Forrester's, I think it's called. Never go there. Dreadful place. The cake was dry. Anyway, I asked the girl how she was still on her feet, considering she'd been working the night before at the Lodge and she literally went as white as a ghost. She mumbled something about not having been working and served me a ghastly rainbow-frosted cupcake. I don't know why she was so shirty about it, I honestly just assumed she was a staff member Suzy hired under my nose."

Lacey was stunned. She managed to whisper a thank you, then ended the call.

Lucia.

Lucia?

Really?

Had she been an accomplice? But why? What on earth could she have against the mayor?

Lacey put her cell phone away. Whatever anxiety she'd felt about speaking to Grumpy Greg, she now felt it tenfold over the fact she was going to need to speak to Lucia.

She got out of the car and headed to the patisserie.

CHAPTER TWENTY

"Lacey!" Tom exclaimed as she walked into the patisserie. It was busy, as normal, with a bunch of children sitting at the window table munching on gingerbread cookies shaped like airplanes. "What are you doing here?" he added, coming out from behind the counter, wiping his hands onto his flour-stained apron, and kissing her cheek.

"I was wondering if Lucia wanted to go for afternoon tea," Lacey said, peering past him to the kitchen where she could hear the clatter of pans and someone humming along to the radio.

Tom beamed. "Really? Oh, Lacey, I'm so pleased. Luce has been desperate to get to know you better. I was starting to think you had something against her."

He chuckled like the thought was ludicrous. Lacey, of course, knew better.

She forced a smile. "Well, I've been super busy, remember? But then I realized, when am I not? I figured it was about time."

"This is perfect. Luce could really do with some downtime," Tom said. "I know the extravaganza at the weekend was extra to her normal hours, but I didn't think I was working her that hard. The poor girl looks exhausted."

"Does she now ...?" Lacey muttered under her breath, her suspicions increasing. Exhausted because of the terrible toll of the secret she'd been keeping?

"Hey, Luce!" Tom called toward the kitchen.

The girl's face popped into view. Tom was right, she looked like she hadn't slept in days. There were dark circles beneath her eyes, and a slightly vacant look in them, like her mind was elsewhere. Lacey collected all the red flags and stored them away in her mind.

"I'm giving you a break," Tom added, as Lucia approached him. He gestured to Lacey. "Lacey wants to take you out for tea."

"Really?" Lucia said, a sudden hopeful glint lighting in her eyes.

Lacey couldn't help but grimace. Why was Lucia *really* so eager to get to know her? To go on the charm offensive and throw Lacey off the trail? To keep her enemy close?

"Yes, really," Lacey confirmed, forcing her face into a friendly smile.

"You don't mind?" Lucia asked Tom. She sounded like a kid asking their parent if they were allowed to go and play with a friend, rather than an employee speaking to her boss. "You're not too busy here?"

"I have a whole stack of gingerbread cookies to keep that lot happy for hours," Tom said, nodding at the party of kids. "You two run along and have fun."

Lucia quickly removed her apron and grabbed her purse. "Thank you!"

Lacey flashed Tom a smile, then headed out the patisserie.

"Where shall we go?" Lucia asked brightly once they were out on the cobblestones.

"How about the tearoom?" Lacey said, gesturing to the closest quaint cafe, two doors down from Tom's. There was no need to drag this out. The sooner she had Lucia cornered the better.

"Okay," Lucia said with an oblivious shrug, following Lacey. She seemed to have really perked up since Tom had allowed her to go on an impromptu break. Perhaps she was faking having energy so Lacey wouldn't question her fatigue.

As they headed toward the tearoom, Lacey caught sight of Gina in the window of the antiques store looking furious. Clearly, she'd misunderstood what was going on and thought Lacey had just lied to her about continuing the investigation in order to sneak off and have a tea break. There was no time to explain everything now; Lacey would just have to leave Gina to stew for the time being.

The tearoom smelled of toast and cinnamon. Lacey ordered them a pot of breakfast tea to share, then came and plonked it on the bistro table Lucia had chosen to sit at.

"I'm so glad we're having our friend date," Lucia said as Lacey took the seat opposite her. "It's just a shame we can't meet up all three of us yet. Poor Suzy. I hope this stuff is over and done with soon."

"Me too," Lacey said, stirring the tea leaves in the pot with a spoon. "I wonder, though, if you might have some information that could help speed the investigation along a little." She leaned forward and slowly began filling her teacup.

"Me?" Lucia asked.

Through the rising steam, she looked innocent enough. But Lacey had learned the hard way with Brooke that looks could be deceiving.

"I've been asking everyone," Lacey said in an attempt to reassure her. "And you were there when it happened, weren't you?" She smiled and switched to pouring tea into her own mug.

"I was in the garden at the time," Lucia replied. "Watching the fireworks."

Lacey took her time pouring the tea. "Were you? I heard you were working for Suzy on Friday night, and that you were down in the basement fetching wine at the time of the murder."

Finally, she flicked her gaze from the tea to Lucia, keeping her expression neutral.

The girl's face had paled. "Who told you that?"

Now she looks rattled, Lacey thought. She gently put down the teapot with a clink. "Does it matter?"

Lucia looked agitated. Her eyes darted around the room almost as if she were looking for an escape route. Of course, there was none. Lacey had made sure to sit between the girl and the door.

Finally, Lucia made eye contact with Lacey again. She looked to be on the verge of tears. "Please don't do this."

Lacey could feel her stomach swirling with nervous dread. On the outside, she kept her cool exterior. "Don't do what?"

"Ruin my life."

Lacey blinked. Her heart was starting to race. She didn't know what to say to that.

Lucia dropped her face into her hands, looking ashamed. "How stupid of me to think you wanted to get to know me," she said bitterly, her words directed at the flowery tablecloth. "You only invited me here to try and catch me out."

Lacey could feel her heart pounding in her chest. It sounded like Lucia was on the verge of confessing. Lacey just had to nudge her over the line. "You make it sound like a game. This is serious, Lucia."

"I know!" the girl wailed, tipping her head up to the ceiling. "I never set out to hurt anyone. I promise. It was just about the money."

Lacey could feel her eyebrows trying to dart together and fought to keep her expression neutral. "Someone paid you?"

"Suzy did, of course."

A hard lump formed in Lacey's throat. "Suzy?"

"Well, it was hardly going to be Greg, was it?" Lucia continued. She shook her head. A silver tear threaded its way down her cheek. "I know you have to tell. But please know we never set out to deceive Tom."

Lacey froze. Tom? What did any of this have to do with her beau? Her mind started turning.

She stared at the girl sitting before her, weeping, her expression creased with torment.

"Why don't you get everything off your chest?" Lacey prompted.

Lucia bit her lip. Then she nodded slowly.

Lacey could hardly believe it. Was she really going to confess that easily?

"Suzy knew I was struggling for money," Lucia began. She laughed sadly. "Let's face it, it's been that way since we first met. Me, the poor kid from the rough bit of town; her, the rich kid in the manor. She always promised me she'd help me get on my feet when the time came. Then I got the job with Tom. She was happy for me. But I guess old habits die hard. When she told me she was opening up the B&B, that's when she made me the proposition."

Lacey was stunned. Appalled. The two had planned Mayor Fletcher's murder? "You...you planned everything from the get-go?"

Lucia nodded. "Suzy didn't know anyone else who lived in Wilfordshire. I was the only person she trusted to help." She looked suddenly worried. "Except for you, of course. I'm sure she would've trusted you as well, but you were already too busy."

Lacey almost choked. "Busy? Busy isn't the issue here! I have *morals*!" She lowered her voice to a hiss-whisper. "I would NEVER help a killer!"

Silence fell.

Across the table from her, Lucia's expression of turmoil disappeared in an instant. Instead, she looked like Lacey had just slapped her in the face. Guilt and shame had made way for anger.

After a protracted silence, Lucia finally spoke. "What do you think we're talking about?"

Lacey replied in the same hushed hiss as before. "You! Accepting money from Suzy to help her murder the mayor! Sneaking into the basement and cutting the lights so Suzy could shoot him under the cover of darkness!"

Another long silence passed. Lucia sucked her cheeks in, her fingers tapping against the lip of her teacup. "I didn't help Suzy plan a murder," she said, her voice now bitterly cold.

"You just admitted it," Lacey replied, pulling her cell phone out of her pocket.

"What are you doing?" Lucia asked.

"Calling the detectives."

Lucia grabbed Lacey's cell phone and slammed it on the tabletop. It was so sudden, Lacey jumped in her seat, and people at the tables nearby turned to look at them.

"I was working for her," Lucia said. "I had a side job, working nights at the B&B! I wasn't a bloody murderer's accomplice!"

Lacey felt her cheeks grow hot with embarrassment. She was more confused than ever.

Had they really been talking at cross-purposes this whole time? Had this all been a huge misunderstanding? But why was Lucia so distressed over Lacey finding out she'd taken on a second job for Suzy?

Lacey's mind raced as she struggled to comprehend how she'd made such a huge error. It had been Lucia's reaction; begging her not to ruin her life! How was working a second job in any way going to do that?

Then Lacey remembered. Tom. Lucia had said right at the beginning of their conversation that she'd never set out to deceive him. She must've thought Lacey would tattle and get her fired.

"Hold on one second," Lacey said, shaking her head. "Is this whole thing about you feeling like you'd betrayed Tom? Because I'm quite certain he'll have no issue with you taking on extra work at all."

Lucia looked suddenly very childlike, hunkering down in her seat like a pupil hauled to the principal's office. Her disproportionate reaction—that taking on a second job would somehow get her into trouble—revealed just how unworldly she really was, and had led Lacey to this incorrect, embarrassing conclusion. Not to mention wasting her time by making her follow an incorrect lead!

"Why would you hide it?" Lacey demanded, her hushed voice now with an edge of frustration. "We're in the middle of a murder investigation! Now isn't the time for secrets."

"Because Tom's been so good to me, training me at the patisserie," Lucia said. "And I probably would've stayed there for years if Suzy hadn't offered me the chance to work at the B&B with her and..."

"Ah," Lacey said, as it dawned on her what Lucia was really confessing. "You're planning on leaving the patisserie."

"Yes," Lucia said, glumly.

"And you didn't trip the lights?"

"No!" She slumped back in her seat. "I can't believe you thought I had something to do with the mayor's murder. I was only fetching bottles of wine from the cellar, because Suzy didn't know if she should trust Greg's staff. All this, just because I'm trying to save money for—"

Lacey stopped her mid-sentence, holding up a hand. "You don't have to explain yourself. I'm really sorry. I was just following the lead. I found out you had access to the basement where the fuse boxes are. You can see why it made me suspicious."

She sighed, realizing she was back at square one.

Except, maybe not completely...

If Suzy had only given access to the basement to people she trusted, then that meant the pool of suspects was still extremely slim. Maybe Lucia could still help.

"Do you know who else Suzy gave access to the basement to?" Lacey asked.

Lucia folded her arms and glared at her. "Really? You're going to accuse me of a crime, then ask for my help? Why should I tell you? So you can go and accuse some other innocent person of being involved in a murder without any proof as well!" She shook her head, looking bitter.

She'd shut down. Lacey had broken the trust between them, and she felt awful for it; not just for being suspicious that the young woman had had a hand in Mayor Fletcher's murder plot, but for *everything*. She'd been so jealous of her. Lucia had only ever wanted to be her friend, and Lacey had been nothing short of hostile toward her. She admitted then to herself that her own insecurities had fueled her suspicions. She'd *wanted* Lucia to be involved so she could have a legitimate reason not to like her. She'd done to her what Gina had done to Brooke. Only Gina had been right in that case. Lacey was just being mean.

She took a deep breath, readying herself for the salvage attempt.

"Lucia, this is for Suzy," she said, firmly but gently. "I need to clear her name. I have every reason to believe that whoever had access to the basement was an accomplice to the murderer. So if you can help, please help. Not for me, but for Suzy."

Lucia twisted her lips. Then she exhaled. "Okay. Fine. Suzy's cousin Mandy went down there as well. I think she was dropping off a cake from her bakery as a gift. It was a cream one and there was no space in the fridge so Suzy said she could take it down to the basement where it was cooler."

Lacey was stunned. Could Suzy's cousin Mandy be the key to everything?

"Listen, Lucia. I'm going to need you to tell me everything you know about Suzy's cousin."

Lucia shrugged. "I don't know her particularly. She runs a bakery in mine and Suzy's hometown."

"What side of the family is she on?"

Lucia drummed her fingers onto the tabletop contemplatively. "You know, I think maybe it's just a nickname. Like she's a longtime family friend so they call her cousin, but I don't think she's a blood relation. They were close enough to spend Christmas together. I remember because I was always really jealous of Suzy's Christmases when we were kids. We'd meet up at the stables and she would tell me about horse riding on snow-covered hillsides and shooting pheasants in old woodlands. It all sounded so quaint."

Lacey slapped her palms down on the table so hard Lucia jumped. "Say that again!"

"It sounded quaint...?"

"No. The pheasants. They went shooting?"

Lucia nodded. "It was a Boxing Day tradition. Suzy's dad is a massive gun nut. He collects ancient ones. I figured that was the inspiration for the Lodge."

Lacey could hardly believe it. Why hadn't Suzy told her about her past when it was so relevant?

Why hadn't she told her about hiring Lucia to work for her the night of the party?

What exactly was she hiding?

Lacey didn't even want to consider that Suzy might have something to do with this after all. But she had access to the gun for the whole week leading up to the murder. She had the expertise to fire it too, according to Lucia. And she was caught holding the gun.

But if it was Suzy, what was her motive?

Just then, Lacey's phone started vibrating on the table, taking her by such surprise she practically jumped out of her skin.

She snatched it up. The name flashing at her was DCI Beth Lewis.

CHAPTER TWENTY ONE

Lacey stared at the detective's name on her phone screen, blinking at it over and over. She and Beth had made a promise to help each other out with the investigation. But now Lacey had just followed a meandering path of evidence all the way back around to Suzy.

What if there was an innocent explanation for her deceit?

But even as she thought it, Lacey realized just how implausible that really was. Suzy had kept secrets from her. It didn't look good for her.

"Aren't you going to answer that?" Lucia prompted from the other side of the table.

Lacey just didn't know what to do. She couldn't hold back what she'd just found out about Suzy. The police needed to know. But Lacey had already made a massive mistake with Lucia. What if she was wrong about Suzy as well? The fallout would be far worse than just a damaged relationship; it would mean prison.

She reached out and hit the red button, rejecting the call. Lacey wasn't going to just hand Suzy over to Detective Lewis without giving her a chance to explain herself first. Even if it meant coming face to face with a killer, Lacey was prepared to do it.

"It can wait," she said to Lucia as she slid the phone back into her pocket.

❧   ❧   ❧

Lacey drove back to Crag Cottage at speed, her mind reeling with the information she'd learned from Lucia.

So Suzy knew how to aim a gun all along; she'd even had a family tradition for shooting. Added to that was the fact that her father was an antique gun collector. She may well have learned from him how to load the flintlock rifle. Then the real nail in the coffin, the thing that pointed to her guilt more than the sum of those things combined: the fact she'd lied by omission. Not just once, either, but over and over and over again. In fact, she'd lied from the very first moment Lacey had shown her the flintlock rifle.

What else had Suzy lied about? Her phobia of dogs? That had vanished somewhat easily!

Lacey felt herself getting more and more riled up as she turned her Rapunzel key in the lock and shoved open the door to Crag Cottage.

"Suzy?" she called into the darkness. "Are you in?"

She was met by silence.

It seemed quiet in the house, Lacey thought. Cold and dark. The old stone cottage seemed to hold onto the chill, so even on a sunny June morning it never quite warmed up. Its small windows and low ceiling didn't help.

Lacey couldn't temper the ominous sense of doom creeping into her. She felt like an intruder in her own home.

"Suzy?" she called again into the darkness.

Again, no answer.

Lacey paced into the kitchen, wondering if maybe Suzy had just gone to her scheduled check-in at the station. But the clock on the wall showed her it was at the middle point between appointments. Suzy ought to be here.

Just then, Lacey saw sudden movement through the window. There was a strange white blur at the end of her garden. Lacey jumped a mile. Her first panicked thought was that there was a ghost on her lawn; her second, coming just a millisecond after it, that it was just one of Gina's sheep. Then, lagging in third place came reality. It was Suzy, facing out toward the cliffs. The thin white summer dress she was wearing was billowing in the ocean wind.

"Get it together," Lacey told herself sternly.

There was no point jumping about imaginary ghosts when she was about to confront a potential killer.

She heaved open the stable door and headed out.

"Suzy?" Lacey called across the large expanse of lawn. Her voice was somewhat swallowed by the wind, and so she made a second attempt to get the young woman's attention. "Suzy?"

This time, the young woman turned and smiled. In the bright beam of sunshine, she looked almost angelic. Lacey had to remind herself she may very well be a murderer, a murderer who'd duped Lacey into a friendship through lies, deceit, and manipulation.

Lacey's stomach swirled as she approached.

"What are you doing home?" Suzy asked, innocently enough. "Is everything okay at the store? Where's Chester?

Now face to face with her, Lacey discovered her mouth had gone completely dry. "Can we talk?" she managed, gesturing for the bench.

"Of course," Suzy said, a slight tremble of concern in her voice as she took it.

"I just had tea with Lucia," Lacey began, sitting beside her.

"You did? That's good!" Suzy gushed. Her brief moment of anxiety seemed to disappear. "It's about time you two got to know each other better. Is that all you wanted to talk to me about?"

She smiled but Lacey couldn't return the gesture. She was too rattled about the conversation she was about to have.

"Lucia told me what happened on Friday evening…" she began, deciding it was best to keep it vague and give Suzy every opportunity to fill in the blanks.

Suzy's face fell instantly. She started wringing her hands fretfully in her lap. "What about Friday?"

Lacey watched her carefully, studying her nervous micro-movements. "I think you know."

Suzy pressed her lips together. Shame flashed behind her eyes. "I'm really sorry, Lacey!" she suddenly blurted, reaching out and grabbing Lacey's hands. "I never planned to go behind yours and Tom's back. Lucia is just so desperate for money and she's too proud to take a loan. She begged me not to tell you about the job."

Lacey had expected Suzy to start there. Maybe the whole poaching Lucia fiasco had only ever been for cover? So that if anyone challenged her she'd have an immediate excuse for her lies?

Lacey took her time answering, making sure she chose her words carefully. She was treading a fine line right now and didn't want to accidentally step over the mark like she'd done with Lucia.

"The thing is," Lacey began, cautiously, "hiring Lucia wouldn't have been a big deal at all if you'd not concealed it from me. It's the fact you hid the truth that hurts."

Suzy chewed her bottom lip. "I know. I'm so sorry. Can you forgive me? Do you feel totally betrayed by me now? I understand if you do. It was a sucky thing for me to do."

Lacey searched Suzy's eyes, trying to see whether her words had actually resonated with her, or whether this was all a carefully composed act. Would Suzy just fall back on youth and inexperience to justify her poor behavior, or would the young woman take the opportunity to confess the rest of her lies?

Suzy shifted, clearly uncomfortable under Lacey's scrutiny. But she kept silent.

"Did you tell the police about Lucia being one of your staff members?" Lacey asked.

"Yes, of course," Suzy said. "I told them everything that was relevant."

"Everything?" Lacey pressed.

Suzy frowned, looking perplexed. "Yes, of course. I'm not going to lie to the police."

She seemed irritable, Lacey thought. Defensive. She could probably sense that Lacey knew *more*. Perhaps it was dawning on her that Lucia had given Lacey more information than just the job situation...

"But you'd lie to me?" Lacey asked.

Suzy fell still. The ocean breeze stirred her hair. Her chest rose and fell deeply, showing an increase in her stress levels. She turned to Lacey. "Lucia told you about my background, didn't she?"

Lacey thought about her shooting abilities, the vital skill Mayor Fletcher's killer would need. "She did."

Suzy nodded somberly and looked ahead, squinting in the sun's glare. "It was just a white lie at first. I only thought you were going to be my decorator. But you were so encouraging when everyone else was so mean. You were supportive. You kept telling me I was capable."

Lacey's heart started to pound. If Suzy was about to blame her *friendship* on the murder she would be furious!

"I thought if you found out I was just a proxy for my parents, you'd lose respect for me."

"A proxy?" Lacey asked.

She nodded. A tear rolled down her cheeks, glittering in the sunshine. "My parents didn't give me the B&B. I'm just the manager."

Lacey's mind turned 180. It was too much to take in.

"That's it?" she stammered. "That's the lie?"

"Once I started, I didn't know how to go back and undo it all. That's why I had to put up with Grumpy Greg. He's worked for my dad for years. And he was mad about rushing to get everything done because I left it so late to start doing the renovation work. I was supposed to start organizing it way sooner but I was too busy with my degree. And naive. I thought it would be easy." She turned her sorrowful face toward Lacey.

Lacey's mind started racing. Suzy was innocent. She had nothing to do with the murder at all. Cousin Mandy was the accomplice, but it hadn't been Suzy she was working for, it had been one of the other Drawing Room Five.

"Suzy, this is important," she said, hurriedly. "Are you absolutely certain that you told the police everything?"

"Yes," the girl said, picking up on Lacey's sudden change of pace and looking worried. "Of course."

"Including who had access to the staff areas of the B&B?"

"Yes!"

"Everyone? Including Cousin Mandy?"

"*Mandy?*" Suzy said. "What on earth has Mandy got to do with anything?"

She looked genuinely surprised.

"You gave her access to the basement," Lacey said.

"So? She wasn't a staff member. She just popped down there to leave a cake."

She didn't seem to understand the significance of the basement, or why whoever had access to it was of such importance.

"The fuse box for the lights are down there," Lacey explained. "It was on the schematics. With all the building and design work you signed off on."

"I told you," Suzy said, "all I am is the B&B's manager. I didn't sign off on anything. I just faxed everything to my dad in Switzerland and got him to sign it all. I didn't even look at the schematics."

"Fine. But you must know that fuse boxes are almost always in the basement."

Suzy shrugged. "I just finished uni. I've never even seen a fuse box. I've never needed to."

"Suzy," Lacey said firmly. "The lights were cut during the fireworks show. The only way they were cut was if someone went into the basement. That someone is the killer's accomplice."

Suzy gasped as understanding came over her.

"The only people who had access to the basement were you, Lucia, and..."

"...Cousin Mandy," Suzy finished, her voice suddenly losing its strength. "Lacey, no!" She started shaking her head. "Mandy can't have anything to do with this. I've known her my whole life. I mean, she's more like family to me than Joanie is. Even if she's only Joanie's half-sister, she always acted more like an aunt to me. And she stuck around after Uncle Adrian's divorce, unlike Joanie, who basically disowned us and dropped out of my life until I moved back to open the B&B! It can't have been Mandy. And besides, she only stopped by for a minute to say hello and give me the cake. She left before the fireworks even started!"

"Are you sure?" Lacey asked. "Did you see her leave? Because there were hundreds of people there, and you couldn't have kept track of everyone. Maybe Mandy said she was leaving and then went down into the basement and waited until the fireworks show?"

Suzy's eyes were starting to well with tears. "I can't bear it. Why would Mandy want to help someone kill Mayor Fletcher? Someone who tried to set me up for the crime? If she did it, she must've been black-mailed into it or something. Mandy would never in her right mind back-stab me like that. She wouldn't lie to me. And what about Carol?" she bellowed. She was starting to sound desperate now. "I thought Carol was the prime suspect, wasn't she? Maybe she found her way into the basement somehow."

Lacey shook her head. "I don't think ..."

But Suzy was on a roll, with passionate tears rolling down her cheeks. "We all know how opposed Carol is to Mayor Fletcher! To the B&B! I mean, she was *furious* when she found out we were opening the shooting club again."

Lacey felt a ripple of disquiet go through her.

"The shooting club?" she asked.

"As part of the regeneration project. My parents, Uncle Adrian, and Aunt Joanie owned it before. I guess it was closed because of the divorce."

Just then, the sound of the garden gate made both women jump.

They turned.

Superintendent Turner was standing there, a triumphant grin on his face. DCI Lewis stood beside him looking sheepish. Lacey could tell by the look on her face that their investigation had led them along the exact same trail as Lacey, that she'd ended up at the place where Suzy had failed to tell the police about Cousin Mandy going into the basement, giving Superintendent Turner the extra bit of evidence he needed.

"I'm sorry," DCI Lewis said, shaking her head.

"Susannah Rowe," Superintendent Turner said, marching forward and producing a pair of handcuffs from his back pocket. "I'm arresting you on suspicion of the murder of Mayor William Fletcher."

"Stop!" Lacey cried, as the cuffs around Suzy's wrists clicked into place. "You know you've got the wrong person!"

The detectives ignored her pleas and began leading Suzy toward the garden gate. Lacey tailed them, following them out through the gate and into the road, where the police car was waiting.

At the sight of it, Suzy started weeping in earnest. "Lacey, help!" she squeaked.

Lacey darted forward, forming a barrier between the officers guiding Suzy and the car they were planning on depositing her.

"You can't do this," she said firmly. "You don't have enough evidence."

Superintendent Turner stared down at her and grinned triumphantly. "I have one Mandy Humphreys sitting in police custody right now. Her perfect, clear fingerprint matches one found on the fuse box in the basement. We know she was Suzy's accomplice."

"But you don't have the prints for Suzy!" Lacey contested.

"I don't need them," Turner said. "Another half hour in the interrogation room with my best boys on her case, and I'm sure Mandy will divulge to us all the evidence we need."

Lacey was getting nowhere with Superintendent Turner. She faced DCI Lewis. She was always the more reasonable of the two. Perhaps she'd see reason.

"Beth, please!" Lacey pleaded. "You *know* it's not Suzy."

Beth kept her gaze averted, but her expression turned to genuine upset. "Oh, I know all right," she hissed. Finally, she turned her focus to Lacey, and daggers practically flew from her eyes. "But thanks to you withholding what you'd learned, I had no way of getting ahead of Turner!"

Lacey felt her stomach sink. This was her fault. "I can explain—"

"Did you have any intention of helping me at all?" Beth butted in before she got the chance. "I thought you had my back."

Lacey felt awful. There were no words to explain that she'd thought the detective might've been double-crossing her that wouldn't add insult to injury.

Just then, the sound of a revving engine made everyone turn. Tom's van was coming racing up the road. It screeched to a halt behind the police car, angled in an odd manner so as to block them in, and Tom leapt out from the driver's seat. He was swiftly followed by the dogs, and Gina bellowing, "You leave that poor girl alone!"

But it was no use. Superintendent Turner ignored the intruders, his face remaining entirely blank as if they weren't even there. He shoved past the dogs yapping at his legs, pulled open the back door of the cruiser, and guided Suzy inside with a hand on her head. DCI Lewis walked around the back of the car to the passenger's side, her eyes down, as if trying to avoid the whole ugly unfolding scene entirely.

"Please!" Lacey said, appealing to her one last time. "You know this is wrong. Mandy was working with someone else. Suzy didn't even know the fuses were in the basement."

DCI Lewis paused at the open car door and gave her a long, disappointed look. For a brief second, Lacey thought she'd gotten through to her. But then the woman sighed.

"Your friend should move his van out of the way or he'll be slapped with a fine for interrupting police procedure. Karl's in that kind of mood."

It was too late. Suzy was in the back of the car, looking younger and more timid than ever.

Gina put an arm around Lacey. "You did your best, chick," she said.

"I let her down."

They watched the car drive away.

❧   ❧   ❧

Lacey sank down at the kitchen table, her head slumping into her hands, her shoulders sagging with defeat.

"I'm sorry, my love," Tom said, coming to her side. He rubbed her back tenderly. "You did everything you could."

Gina took the seat opposite her and leaned forward, giving her forearms a firm yet affectionate squeeze.

"What am I supposed to do now?" Lacey stammered. "With Suzy in custody there's no way I'll be able to make my credit card payments. I'll default on my mortgage payment to Ivan. My rent at the store. I'll have to close down."

Gina and Tom exchanged a glance. Clearly, neither had realized just how dire the situation had become for Lacey, that saving Suzy wasn't just some moral crusade she was on, but something that had very real, devastating implications for her as well.

"Let me call my mom," Tom said. "She might have some suggestions."

Lacey was too dejected to protest, even though confessing her near-bankruptcy to Heidi Forrester wasn't exactly going to do much for her already tarnished reputation.

Tom paced away to call his mom, and Lacey felt Chester shoving against her legs under the table. She looked down at him, at his big trusting brown eyes, and felt a hitch of emotion in her chest.

"I failed," she told him, petting him. "I failed."

He let out a sad whine and sank his head into her lap.

Tom returned to them, placing his phone on the center of the table. "Go ahead, Mom. You're on speakerphone."

Through the speaker came Heidi's voice. "Lacey, I'm sorry about your predicament. Tom explained everything. I'm afraid that I must be the bearer of bad news. There's not a lot to be done now, I'm afraid. Any defense at this point would be a shot in the dark."

She continued speaking, but Lacey tuned her voice out. Repeating over and over like a stuck record, drowning out all other sounds, were the words *"a shot in the dark. A shot in the dark. A shot in the dark ..."*

"I've got it," she suddenly exclaimed.

Tom and Gina looked at her, perplexed. Heidi abruptly stopped speaking, leaving her sentence unfinished.

But Lacey was too wrapped in the moment to think about how rude she'd been in shouting over Heidi, and how such behavior wouldn't have curried her any more favors. She was on her feet, grabbing for her car keys.

"I know what happened!" she cried to Tom and Gina, who were looking like her sudden change in mood had left them both with whiplash. "We need to get to the Lodge now. I can prove it. Come on!"

Chester barked his support, and for the first time in ages, Lacey felt suddenly hopeful.

CHAPTER TWENTY TWO

"**A**re you sure we're allowed to be back here?" came Tom's voice from somewhere behind Lacey as she closed the gate behind them.

She turned back to face Gina, Tom, Boudica, and Chester, all standing patiently in the large garden of the Lodge, four gloomy figures in the fading light.

"Yup," she said, because the garden wasn't technically the crime scene. "Just keep to the walls so we don't set off the burglar lights."

She took the lead. Behind, she could hear their footsteps in the soft grass, and their clothes scraping against the brick wall as they hugged it.

"Okay, now I'm pretty sure you're lying," Tom said again. "If we're allowed to be here, why are we creeping in the shadows? And what are we even looking for?"

Lacey reached the coal bunker doors, a hatch-like entrance that actually gave them access into the cellar. She remembered seeing it on the schematics.

She slid the bolt across and gave the handles a tug. The doors opened with a clunk.

"We're going into the B&B?" Tom asked. "Are you crazy? That's trespassing! We'll get arrested!"

Lacey shushed him. "No we won't. Just be quiet. We don't want anyone to catch us ... yet."

Since DCI Lewis hadn't answered any of Lacey's frantic calls, she'd been forced to come up with a slightly more creative solution. She was going to lure the detective to her.

She ushered everyone down the steps—the dogs excited, Gina enthusiastic, and Tom reluctant—and into the dark bunker. It was dark, and Lacey had to scrabble around to find the access door that would take them to the wine cellar.

"This way," Lacey whispered.

They went through the door into the wine cellar, Lacey using her memory of the schematics to guide them toward the concrete steps that would lead them into the B&B's corridor. She found them, noting just how closely positioned to them the fuse boxes were. It could've taken the accomplice as little as ten seconds to zip down here and cut the lights.

They climbed the concrete steps, and Lacey pressed her finger to her lips before she opened the adjoining door and led them into the B&B's corridor.

It was very cold inside the B&B. It felt empty and unloved. Without people passing through, the smell of the antique wood furnishings had been given a chance to permeate into the air.

Lacey ducked behind the reception desk, then glanced along the corridor for any signs of officers since Beth had told her before that the place would be guarded. She couldn't see anyone, so she tiptoed as far as the glass doors that led to the foyer.

She tipped her head round the corner and could just make out the figure of a single police officer guarding the main entrance to the building. What a stroke of luck! They must've needed all hands on deck back at the station to help with the interrogations of Mandy and Suzy.

Suzy ... Lacey thought, her stomach twisting in anguish for her friend. She used it to fuel her onwards.

Checking through the foyer, Lacey saw the officer was facing away, so she quickly beckoned to Tom and Gina that the coast was clear.

They came out from behind the reception desk, the dogs following their heels, and hurried past where Lacey was crouched by the foyer doors safely to the other side of the corridor. Then it was Lacey's turn. She made another quick check to ensure the officer was still not looking, then hurried past herself.

"Okay, this way," she whispered, leading them toward the Drawing Room door. She tugged the police tape from off the door.

"I don't like this," Tom said. "Not one bit."

"Neither do I," Lacey replied.

But she had no other choice. She was absolutely certain that the evidence to prove which of the Drawing Room Five had killed him was hidden inside. This was the only way to clear Suzy's name and nail the real murderer.

She pushed open the door and went inside. A chill ran up her spine as her gaze fell automatically to the place where Mayor Fletcher had died.

"Okay, everyone, you know what you're looking for." She crouched down, peering under the couch. "We'd better be quick before we get caught."

"Too late for that," she heard a male voice say. "Police. Stand up slowly. Hands where I can see them."

Lacey raised herself to her feet and found herself squinting into the glare of a flashlight. She slowly hands in the air.

Her eyes flickered to the left, to where Tom was standing in the same position. The white glare of the light had turned him into a glowing angel, with the bronze copper coal bucket beside him looking like glittering gold.

"I told you we weren't allowed to be here," Tom said in a less than angelic tone.

Lacey looked over to Gina on her right, with Boudica cowering at her feet. Just as she wondered what had happened to her own pup, Chester nudged his way past her and began to growl at the officer.

"Quiet, boy," Lacey commanded, nervous for the first time that a growling dog might panic the officer into action.

He obeyed her, falling silent.

"You're trespassing," came the officer's disembodied voice from behind the blindingly bright flashlight.

"We are," Lacey said confidently. "In fact, we're not just trespassing, but we're meddling with a crime scene."

"Uhhh ... Lacey?" came Tom's trembling voice from her left shoulder.

Lacey ignored him. She knew what she was doing. "You probably should call your supervisor. She'll want to know."

There was a moment of hesitation. Then Lacey heard the distinct click of a walkie-talkie speaker being pressed, followed by the static noise of it connecting.

"DCI Lewis," the officer's voice murmured. "Ma'am, we have trespassers at the Lodge. Two women, one man, and...two dogs."

A crackled reply came immediately. Though Lacey couldn't hear the words clearly, she could make out that the voice was female.

Suddenly, the flashlight beam went out, and the standing lamp beside the door was turned on. The room filled with a warm yellow glow, and Lacey saw the ginger-haired police officer who'd questioned her in the kitchen was standing beside it. He had a perplexed expression, as he unclipped his speaker from his right shoulder and held it out to Lacey, eyeing her warily.

"She says she wants to talk to you."

Lacey took the speaker and pressed the button at the side.

"Go ahead, Beth," she said.

"Lacey," came the detective's weary voice. "What are you doing?"

"I tried to call but you didn't answer, so I had to get creative. I know what happened to Mayor Fletcher."

She let go of the button and listened to the static while she waited for the detective's response.

Finally, DCI Lewis replied. "Do you have evidence?"

"Yes," Lacey replied, confidently. She didn't have it *yet* but while the officer had been shining his flashlight in her face, she'd worked out exactly where she would find it. "I know who killed Mayor Fletcher and I know how to prove it. I suggest you send people out to escort the Drawing Room Five here. You can bring Suzy with you. Oh, and you're going to need an evidence bag."

There was a long staticky pause on the other end of the line.

"Fine," DCI Lewis said. Not even the distortion from the speaker could hide the fact she was obviously speaking between clenched teeth. "Just don't touch anything. Please. If you contaminate the evidence it won't be admissible in court. We'll be there in five."

Lacey handed back the speaker to the surprised-looking officer and smiled pleasantly.

"My friends and I are going to put our hands down now, okay?"

CHAPTER TWENTY THREE

Ivan was the first to arrive. He entered the drawing room behind his police escort, wearing the same troubled expression he had the day Lacey bumped into him in the street.

"Can someone please tell me why I'm here?" he asked, nervously, his eyes darting from the officers to the dogs to Lacey, Tom, and Gina standing beside the fireplace.

"Detective Lewis will be here shortly," the ginger-haired police officer said. "She'll explain everything in due time."

He side-eyed Lacey, as if to say, *"She better bloody do."* Lacey kept her chin up high and her resolve firm.

From down the corridor came the sound of a woman furiously monologuing.

"Sounds like Carol's here," Gina said, hiding her smile behind her hand.

The door opened again and in came a very stressed-looking officer, accompanying Carol, who was red in the face and puffing and panting.

"What in God's name is this all about?" she blustered, taking in the sight of the people inside the room.

"They won't say," Ivan told her, meekly.

"Didn't you ask?" Carol bellowed. "I'm quite certain it's against the law to escort someone to an undisclosed location for an unspecified reason!"

"Detective Lewis will explain everything once she arrives," the ginger-haired officer said dispassionately.

Lacey watched as the exasperated officer who'd landed the unfortunate task of escorting Carol here sidled up to the ginger-haired policeman and asked out the side of his mouth, "What's going on?"

The ginger-haired man just shook his head and glowered at Lacey.

Once again, the door opened. But rather than anyone coming in, nothing but a shiny shoe poked into the room, accompanied by the commanding voice of Councilor Muir as she said, "What do you mean my aide can't come in with me? They're with me at all times. They have to wait outside?"

Lacey couldn't hear the voice of the officer the councilor was presumably arguing with standing in the doorway over her shoulder. But she did hear the moment Councilor Muir gasped and exclaimed, "Adrian? What are you...? Why is...? What on earth is going on?!"

The door was shoved open fully and Councilor Muir stormed inside. She was followed by her police escort and, notably, no aide. She looked around the room with displeasure at the sight awaiting her; the officers, the other suspects, the dogs, and of course, her ex-husband, who'd followed in quietly after her.

"What is this?" she demanded, hands on hips. Then, before the ginger officer even had a chance to trot out the party line, she pointed a finger at his face and said, "I am going to sue you lot. And I'll have your super fired. Where is he anyway?"

"*She* is right behind you," DCI Lewis said.

Everyone's focus switched from Councilor Muir to Detective Lewis as she entered with Suzy in tow.

While everyone clambered to get the detective's attention, Suzy flashed Lacey a sad but hopeful smile. Lacey gave her a reassuring nod.

"Settle down!" Detective Lewis said, raising her hands, and the volume of her voice, in order to restore order. "I know this is a bit different than usual police procedure—"

"I'll say!" Councilor Muir interrupted rudely. "I have a tight schedule to adhere to."

"We all do, Joan," Ivan said in an unassumingly assured way.

The councilwoman folded her arms and fell silent.

"As I was saying," Beth continued, "you're the five witnesses who were in the room when Mayor Fletcher was shot." Anyone who didn't know her well would assume she was telling the truth. But Lacey could recognize the tell-tale signs on the woman's face that showed she was bending it a little to fit the situation. "We've decided it will help the investigation to physically reposition you all to get a ... visual representation of the night."

She was clearly struggling for words. Behind her, Lacey could see the officers subtly exchanging confused glances.

Just then, the door opened once more and Superintendent Turner waltzed in. Beth paled.

"I heard there was a show," he said coldly to Beth. "My invitation must've gotten lost in the mail." He walked over to Lacey and handed her a slip of paper. "That's a fine for trespassing." He smiled nastily, then walked over to the other officers and said, "Please. On with the show."

Beth looked nervously at Lacey. But Lacey wasn't rattled. She couldn't care less about being fined for trespassing, or about Superintendent Turner's attempts to show her up. She was here to prove her theory.

"If everyone could take their places," Beth Lewis said hurriedly.

The five suspects looked reticent as they shuffled around the room into the positions they were in on the night of the murder. Adrian looked the most uncomfortable; the bullet hole the rifle had made was right there in the wooden sideboard beside him.

Once everyone was in place, DCI Lewis nodded to Lacey, as if to say, *"Over to you."*

Lacey stepped toward the semicircle of suspects.

"Who among you had means and motive to murder Mayor Fletcher? Carol?" She stopped next to the woman. "Motive, yes. A very public one, in fact. She hated Mayor Fletcher for the regeneration project that would, in her opinion, destroy the character of the town. She brought Fairy Liquid to the party in an attempt to sabotage it, so she's obviously a grudge holder. And she confessed to shutting the curtains in the drawing room, claiming her photosensitivity was the reason. But did she have the means? Could she load, aim, and fire an antique rifle in the dark? No."

She stepped past Carol, whose chest sank with an expelled breath, and drew up beside Ivan. He gulped.

"What about Ivan? Ivan had motive. He'd lost a bunch of money because of Mayor Fletcher. But did he shoot the gun? No. Because Ivan is afraid of the dark. He'd never choose to plunge a room into darkness that way."

She carried on along the line. "And Suzy? She had the means—access to the weapon and the skills to fire it—but what was her motive? She had none."

She passed Suzy and stopped beside Councilor Muir. "Councilor Muir had the means, too. A connection to Wilfordshire's old shooting club. But her supposed motive to take the mayor's job doesn't hold up. They were far from rivals. They were friends. The last thing Councilor Muir wanted to do was shoot Mayor Fletcher."

Lacey paced onwards, crossing the distance from the end of the semicircle of suspects to the final man. Uncle Adrian. She stopped beside the tall man and let out a sigh. "Because she wanted to shoot Adrian."

Everyone gasped.

Lacey swirled on the spot back to Councilor Muir, pointing a finger of accusation at her.

"Mayor Fletcher wasn't the target!" she accused. "Your ex-husband, Adrian, was the target all along!"

The room erupted into hubbub. Adrian grabbed the bar to steady himself. It looked like his legs might give up under him.

"This is preposterous!" Councilor Muir cried. "How exactly did you come to such a ludicrous conclusion?"

"I was wondering the same thing myself," Superintendent Turner said, stepping toward Lacey. "If you don't hurry this up, I'm taking you to the station and putting your little dog in the pound."

Lacey caught Beth Lewis's eye. The woman looked surprised but intrigued, and gave her a nod of reassurance.

Lacey stepped forward.

"I met you on the day you came to drop off Suzy's business license. You went to great pains to stress that you were Suzy's *ex*-aunt. I thought it was because you were uncomfortable about expediting the business license. But it was more than that, wasn't it? You told me you were her ex-aunt because you literally were; you stopped acting like an aunt to her ten years ago when you disowned Adrian's entire family. Before the divorce, you'd spent every Christmas going on shooting trips together. You'd even run a business with Adrian and his brother and wife. The divorce might have been amicable if Adrian hadn't lost—how much was it you said at the party?—three hundred thousand pounds due to financial mismanagement. Of course, for the rest of the Rowe family three hundred thousand pounds was barely a blip on their radar. But for you, it was a huge deal. You let your hatred toward Adrian turn into hatred for his whole family."

Superintendent Turner was clearly finding it very difficult to remain patient. He stepped toward Lacey and said loudly, "Are you honestly accusing someone whose motive to commit murder is a decade old?"

"A decade old but freshly re-awoken," Lacey said right back without missing a beat. She looked back at Councilor Muir and continued. "Ten years ago you'd distanced yourself from the family, but then it all got dragged back up again by your ex-brother-in-law's plan to turn his retirement home into a B&B and restart the shooting club business. That must have grated on you, hearing about that again, knowing you'd lost all that money and now the club was coming back without you. At some point, you realized this might be your opportunity to bring down Adrian and the rest of his family in one go.

"You saw the rifle and started formulating a plan. Adrian would visit the B&B at some point, it was just a case of having everything in place for the moment when your paths finally crossed. So you were friendly enough to Suzy that she'd assume bygones were bygones. You bought the ammunition and loaded the rifle—knowing you were a perfect shot and would never miss your target, but also knowing you could feign ignorance that the rifle was loaded. Then, luckily for you, you only had to wait a few days. Adrian was coming to the party. It was a little risky to do it somewhere with so many people present, but you found a way to use that to your advantage. The fireworks display would lure most people into the garden, except for Adrian who you knew cared more for networking than fireworks, and would be orbiting around Mayor Fletcher, who you knew would be sampling whisky by the bar all night. If there was anyone else in the room, they'd all be at the window watching the display anyway. But just to be on the safe side, you persuaded Mandy to cut the electricity when the fireworks began. That would give you just enough time and just enough light to grab the rifle and fire. But it didn't quite pan out that way, did it? Because Carol had closed the curtains, and when the lights cut off, you were plunged into complete darkness. You had to improvise. You figured you were a good enough shot to pull it off, so you took a shot in the dark, shoving the gun into your niece's hands to frame her. But there were tragic consequences to your gamble. You missed the target and killed your friend."

The room fell into stunned silence.

"Joan . . ." Adrian stammered, his voice etched with agony. "Is it true? Did you really want me dead?"

Suzy ran to her uncle, clasping his hand in hers.

"Auntie Joanie!" she wailed. "How could you?"

Councilor Muir looked at them both. "Please. Of course I didn't! That's not what happened at all. Don't be silly."

But Ivan shook his head sadly. "Give it up, Joan. I suspected you from the get-go, but I just didn't want to believe it. When Lacey pointed out over breakfast that the killer would need to be a skilled gunman to know how to load and fire an antique weapon, that was the nail in the coffin."

"You suspected me from the get-go?" Councilor Muir said, sounding offended.

Ivan hung his head in shame. "You passed me to take the gun off the wall."

"It was pitch-black. That could have been anyone!"

"I know your perfume, Joan," Ivan said, sounding like the hopeless recipient of unrequited love. "I'd recognize it anywhere."

"Ivan," Councilor Muir said, her voice softening. "You know I'm not capable of this."

Beth sidled up to Lacey and whispered in her ear. "You said there was evidence."

"There is," Lacey said. "Did you bring gloves for evidence handling?"

Beth exhaled irritation through her nostrils and pulled out a pair of cream latex gloves. Lacey slid them over her hands.

Then she stepped forward and raised her voice to be heard over the din. "Anyone who knows about antique weapons knows they leave gunpowder residue. Which makes beautiful elbow-length black gloves the perfect choice for Councilor Muir to wear that evening." She paced toward the mantelpiece. "I noticed your hands were bare when you were giving Mayor Fletcher CPR."

"I got grease on them from the barbeque!" Councilor Muir exclaimed.

"Oh really?" Lacey said, crouching down beside the bronze coal buckets and shoving her hands inside. "So you didn't take them off after the kill shot and quickly shove them into the coal bucket?"

Lacey pulled her now blackened hands from the bucket and held up two crumpled silky black gloves.

The gasp that went around the room was enormous.

Councilor Muir looked stunned. Her mouth opened as if she was going to make another excuse. But nothing came out.

Then, quick as a flash, she turned on her heel and made a dash for the door.

Everyone in the room was so stunned, they were slow to react. But not Chester. Lacey's trusty companion raced after her and rugby-tackled her to the floor.

"Benson!" Councilor Muir screeched.

Her aide appeared at the door. He looked at the scene of the Councilor lying sprawled face-first on the floor with an English Shepherd dog on her back and his eyes widened with confusion. "I'll call the police!" he exclaimed, before realizing the room was full of them. "No ... I'll call... I'll call ..."

He stopped. For the first time in his employment with Councilor Joan Muir, there was no one to call.

Beth hurried over to where Chester was pinning the murderer to the floor, and jammed a knee into the woman's back, retrieving a pair of cuffs from her hip.

"Joan Muir, you're under arrest for the murder of Mayor Fletcher."

As she clicked the cuffs in place, Beth looked up at Lacey and gave her a nod.

They'd done it.

Epilogue

It was a warm summer evening. Lacey strolled along the beach front with Chester at her side, breathing in the smell of ocean air. Up ahead, she could see light spilling from the open doors of the town hall and hear the sound of chatter coming from inside.

She felt her phone buzz and retrieved it from her pocket.

The message was from Xavier.

Lacey, you must tell me, is everything okay? I have not heard from you since you called me in the middle of the night! What is going on?

She regarded the screen for a moment, reading the message once, and then twice. She didn't quite know how to phrase what she wanted to say in response.

But before she got the chance, she heard thudding footsteps coming up behind her.

"Lacey!" came the breathless voice of Suzy.

Lacey turned and saw her friend racing across the sand toward her. When they met, they embraced, and Chester leapt up, pawing at them.

Suzy laughed. "Yes, hello, dear Chester. I'm happy to see you, too."

"Are you coming to the meeting?" Lacey asked Suzy.

"You bet I am," Suzy said, linking arms with Lacey. "There's going to be an announcement about the Lodge."

"Is there now?" Lacey asked, intrigued.

She slid her phone into her pocket and the two women plus one dog strolled the final few feet to the town meeting.

It was busy inside. Far busier than usual. It seemed as if half of Wilfordshire had decided to come. Then Lacey realized why. This was the first meeting following Mayor Fletcher's death. It was a significant and poignant one to everyone who resided in the town.

Lacey and Suzy took seats together, just in time for Ivan, the speaker of the meeting, to take to the stage.

"Our first order of business," he said, "is to announce that the Lodge has officially opened."

Everyone started clapping, and Lacey leaned over to Suzy with a big grin on her face.

"Is that the announcement?" she asked. "Congratulations."

Suzy squeezed Lacey's arm. "It's all thanks to you. And guess what, we're fully booked for next weekend!"

Lacey smiled. She would make her money back for the stock in no time!

"And," Suzy added, "my guest of honor will be Cousin Mandy."

"She's been released?" Lacey asked, relieved.

Suzy nodded. "The police dropped their charges this morning. They found Joanie's notebook where she planned the murder, and it was right there in black and white, her plan to trick Mandy into turning off the lights during the fireworks display. She'd told her she'd arranged a surprise light show for me and needed someone to trip the fuse."

"Sneaky," Lacey replied.

Suzy nodded. "I knew there was no way Mandy would be involved."

From his position at the pulpit, Ivan continued speaking. "The next order of business is Bill Fletcher's funeral, which is taking place on Tuesday."

He began giving details of the service. As he spoke, Lacey spotted Lucia amongst the audience. She was with a man, and they appeared to be holding hands.

Lacey lent to Suzy and whispered, "Who is that guy with Lucia?"

"Devon," Suzy said. "Her fiancé."

Lacey couldn't believe it. Fiancé? All that time she'd been jealous of Lucia, she'd had a fiancé all along!

"She's not wearing a ring," Lacey whispered.

Suzy shook her head. "They want to go traveling around the world so instead of a big expensive wedding and ring, they're saving up for the trip."

Lacey remembered Lucia trying to tell her she'd taken on extra work to save money for something. It must've been her big world trip with her fiancé.

Lacey decided then and there she wasn't going to be suspicious of Lucia anymore. Jealousy was such a waste of energy.

"Now onto the town mayor nominations," Ivan announced. "We'd like to ask people to nominate their candidates."

"I want to nominate myself," Carol said, standing up.

"You can't do that," Ivan replied. "Someone in the community has to nominate you."

Lacey rolled her eyes and stood. "I'll nominate Carol."

At least give the woman a chance.

Carol looked thrilled. She smirked at Ivan. "There."

"All right," Ivan said, adding her name to a piece of paper.

"I'd also like to nominate you," Lacey said.

Ivan looked up. "I'm sorry. Who?"

"You," Lacey said. "Ivan Parry."

The audience seemed to be in agreement; little noises of approval rippled through the hall.

"Me?" Ivan exclaimed.

"I don't know anyone else who has the town's interests at heart more than you do," Lacey said.

Ivan looked chuffed. "All right then, I'm on the list." He added his name. "That's all for today, folks. Thanks for your attendance."

Everyone stood up and began to filter out of the hall.

"Good luck with Gina tomorrow," Lacey told Suzy as they exited onto the beach. "I'm going to miss having her at the store, but I know she's in safe hands."

Suzy chuckled. "Thanks for lending her to me. I can't wait for her to be Chief Gardener. Oh look, it's Tom."

Lacey glanced up. Her handsome beau was strolling across the sand toward her. She said goodbye to Suzy and approached him. He swept her into his arms.

"What are you doing here?" Lacey asked, giggling.

"I thought it was about time we went on that overdue date," he told her. "Don't you?"

"Absolutely," Lacey said.

Chester barked.

"Yes, you can come too!" Tom said, petting the dog's head. "Oh, there's Lucia and Devon. Mind if I say a quick hello before we leave?"

Lacey smiled. "Be my guest."

As she watched Tom walk over to the others, she took her phone from her pocket. She'd finally worked out what to say to Xavier.

I've decided to take a break in my search for my father. I want to focus on the present right now, rather than the past.

It was a little white lie. Lacey had no intention of scaling back her search for her father, but she was sure she could do it just fine on her own, without Xavier's flirtatious treasure-hunt-style gifts and clues.

Satisfied with her decision, she went to return her phone to her pocket, when it dinged in her hand.

That was quick, Lacey thought, hesitating.

She'd hoped Xavier wouldn't reply immediately, that she'd at least have her date with Tom to distract her from the fallout of her final decision. But then she shook her head and strengthened her resolve. Whatever was contained in Xavier's return message, it would not change her decision. Her mind was made up. No matter how much Xavier attempted to twist her arm, she would stay strong and interpret his response as a line in the sand. A period.

But when she looked down at the glowing screen and read Xavier's message, her resolve shattered into the tiniest of pieces.

Are you sure? Because I have found a very important lead. Lacey, I think I know where your father is.

Now Available!

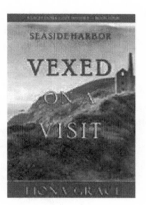

VEXED ON A VISIT
(A Lacey Doyle Cozy Mystery—Book 4)

"Very entertaining. I highly recommend this book to the permanent library of any reader that appreciates a very well written mystery, with some twists and an intelligent plot. You will not be disappointed. Excellent way to spend a cold weekend!"

—Books and Movie Reviews, Roberto Mattos
(regarding *Murder in the Manor*)

VEXED ON A VISIT (A LACEY DOYLE COZY MYSTERY—BOOK 4) is book four in a charming new cozy mystery series by Fiona Grace.

Lacey Doyle, 39 years old and freshly divorced, has made a drastic change: she has walked away from the fast life of New York City and settled down in the quaint English seaside town of Wilfordshire.

Summer has arrived, and Lacey is delighted when her chef boyfriend surprises her with an offer for a long weekend trip, a romantic getaway into the neighboring seaside towns of the British countryside, with her beloved dog, and a chance to go antiquing.

But Lacey is even more surprised when her family shows up from New York on a surprise visit—and when they want to come along!

Even worse, Lacey, in a neighboring town, finds herself in the midst of a murder scene. And once again, with her reputation on the line, she may be the only one who can solve it.

Book #5 is also now available!

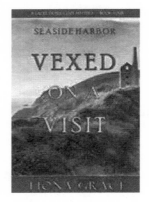

VEXED ON A VISIT
(A Lacey Doyle Cozy Mystery—Book 4)

Also Now Available!
A New Series!

AGED FOR MURDER
(A Tuscan Vineyard Cozy Mystery—Book 1)

"Very entertaining. I highly recommend this book to the permanent library of any reader that appreciates a very well written mystery, with some twists and an intelligent plot. You will not be disappointed. Excellent way to spend a cold weekend!"

—Books and Movie Reviews, Roberto Mattos
(regarding *Murder in the Manor*)

AGED FOR MURDER (A TUSCAN VINEYARD COZY MYSTERY) is the debut novel in a charming new cozy mystery series by #1 bestselling author Fiona Grace, author of Murder in the Manor (Book #1), a #1 Bestseller with over 100 five-star reviews—and a free download!

When Olivia Glass, 34, concocts an ad for a cheap wine that propels her advertising company to the top, she is ashamed by her own work—yet offered the promotion she's dreamed of. Olivia, at a crossroads, realizes this is not the life she signed up for. Worse, when Olivia discovers her long-time boyfriend, about to propose, has been cheating on her, she realizes it's time for a major life change.

Olivia has always dreamed of moving to Tuscany, living a simple life, and starting her own vineyard.

When her long-time friend messages her about a Tuscan cottage available, Olivia can't help wonder: is it fate?

Hilarious, packed with travel, food, wine, twists and turns, romance and her newfound animal friend—and centering around a baffling small-town murder that Olivia must solve—AGED FOR DEATH is an unputdownable cozy that will keep you laughing late into the night.

Books #2 and #3 in the series—AGED FOR DEATH and AGED FOR MAYHEM—are now also available!

AGED FOR MURDER
(A Tuscan Vineyard Cozy Mystery—Book 1)

Made in the USA
Las Vegas, NV
25 August 2023

76575674R00116